HELLO, WORLD!

Mark Rodseth

CONTENTS

ISBN: 9798853961821

For my children, Emilia and Adam.

PREFACE

I had the idea for Hello, World! in 2018, sketched the outline of the book and began writing it. After a few chapters, life got in the way, and I put the book on the shelf to gather dust for a few years.

Fast forward to 2023 and the boom in Artificial Intelligence instigated through Generative AI made me realise that reality was starting to race against my idea. I picked up pen and paper and threw myself into finishing the novel.

New tools at my disposal such as ChatGPT and MidJourney were extremely helpful in the creative process from idea generation, research, evaluation, visual exploration and copy editing.

It was fitting that writing about AI involved taking advantages on new AI tools on the market.

My writing process will never be the same again.

ACKNOWLEDGEMENTS

There are several people who helped me on this journey I would like to thank.

To my wife Kasia for all her support, encouragement and valuable insights and ideas along the way.

To Claude De Guyader who did the first couple rounds of major editing. Claude is an extremely talented editor and has deep knowledge of Japan which was especially useful for this novel.

To Alison Rodseth and her daughters, Emma and Olivia, who did a brilliant job in the final edit and proof reading.

INTRODUCTION

Hello, World! is a near-term sci-fi action thriller where AI research and development takes place in Quantum Sandboxes which serve to contain the risk of opening the Pandora's Box of Superintelligence. A global summit then takes place where a vote is passed to dismantle and ban all AI Research Facilities and Initiatives, as the risk to humanity is too great. This is known as The Shutdown.

Following the ban, a leading scientist who has campaigned against the Shutdown is drafted in by a secret organisation to fight against what is considered by many as our species' greatest mistake. This organisation has the money, the power, the technology and the facility to bring Artificial Intelligence to life.

There is one last Sandbox, where Superintelligence can be developed to its full potential, and where the future of man and machine hang in the balance.

The story takes place in London and Tokyo and is a race between an underground organisation and international government to unleash or to kill the potential of artificial life.

Hello, World! grapples with what it means to be human, the risks and opportunities that AI presents, and the relationships we form with one another and with machines.

And... it's action-packed with lots of cool tech.

PART 1

Victor Bukowski

Then you don't remember a world without robots. There was a time when humanity faced the universe alone and without a friend. Now he has creatures to help him; stronger creatures than himself, more faithful, more useful, and absolutely devoted to him. Mankind is no longer alone.

— I, ROBOT, ISAAC ASIMOV (1950)

Your scientists were so preoccupied with whether or not they could, they didn't stop to think if they should.

— DR. IAN MALCOLM, JURASSIC PARK (1993)

I have no fear of computers. I fear the absence of human beings in their presence.

— RAY BRADBURY (DATE UNKOWN)

CHAPTER 1

Victor's eyes open and reality streams back into his consciousness. Fragmented memories merge, split, and combine again in this fragile and formative moment between sleep and wakefulness.

He struggles into a sitting position at the foot of the bed, rubs his eyes and tries to shake the fuzzy dissociation that comes with time-zone-busting flights. The worst side effect of jet lag for him is the gnawing anxiety that he has lost something or left something behind. Perhaps he has, he muses, his soul tethered to Washington DC and still racing to catch up.

The last two days' events start playing back in his mind.

He failed. Christ, he tried everything, but it wasn't enough.

Forcing the recollections aside, Victor begins his morning stretching routine. His body labours through the movements, not yet grasping it is five in the morning and that it needs to make up for six hours of evaporated time.

Next, coffee. Black. Victor takes a sip and peers out of the window of his second-floor Camden flat which overlooks the narrow street carving through the rows of terraced, beige-brick Victorian houses. Early morning summer light softens its typically stark, grimy appearance.

An autonomous street cleaner glides along the pavement, telescopic arms and brushes working in harmony to clear yesterday's debris. Passersby occasionally appear—heading to work, returning home, or wandering aimlessly, treating Sweeper like a benign ghost.

Victor eventually shifts away and sits down at his workstation. He removes his Cube from the strap on his wrist, places it on the table and waves his hand. The square device's thin hexagonal lines illuminate white before a holographic display is projected in the air and the keys of a keyboard appear displayed onto his desk. An array of windows appears, each with different text and graphical interfaces into his work.

He expands one window, a split screen with the output of his latest Neural Net experiment on the right and the AI agent, colloquially named Murphy, on the left. Victor disappears into his back-and-forth exchange with Murphy, partly verbal, partly keyboard-driven, making micro adjustments, evaluating the effect of each change, and again: fine-tuning, optimising, coercing. The cognitive ballet takes him away from the reality of the Summit, the potential consequences of the 'Yes' vote, and the flood of messages sending condolences.

After a few hours, he resurfaces and heads to Regent's Park for a late-morning jog.

Colourful frantic life has descended on Camden Town. The warm-up walk to the park requires dodging and weaving through Sunday crowds of tourists, locals, beggars, workers, and those on the fringe that Camden attracts to its gothic, electro core.

The crowd eases after Victor passes the Electric Ballroom and turns into Parkway Road. A group of youths sits against the wall of the Jazz Cafe, vaping and tittering to each other, dishevelled and glazed after an all-nighter. The air smells of marijuana, fruity vaping aromas, and fried chicken.

The air in the park is fresh and clean in contrast, infused with freshly cut grass and flowers. The joyful shouts and laughter of children mix in with music drifting from different pockets in the park.

Victor alters his route to circumvent the dense crowds in the centre. He jogs along the perimeter, past social football teams, young couples manoeuvring their strollers, idle youths, and solitary wanderers tracing the asphalt paths. A familiar, hollow pain twists in his gut as he observes harmonious family units. Each shared smile and laugh reminding him of what he once had.

Two Jack Russells dart in front of him, pulling him out of his mental sinkhole, tugging against the leash connected to their hovering Robo-Walkers.

Back at home, Victor dives under a cold shower. Despite the icy water's invigorating sting, the oppressive burden of jet lag bears down on him. He picks at reheated chicken pasta whilst enjoying the deep richness of Miles Davis' Birth Of The Cool. He succumbs to the music, allowing it to artfully smooth his frayed nerves.

On a typical day, he'd launch into another deep work session, but today he braces himself for the reactions and commentary surrounding the Summit vote.

There is much anger online. The vote has created greater polarisation between two extreme views: those who believe AI is a meteor heading for humanity's total destruction, and those who think AI is Bruce Willis on a rocket ship sent to destroy it and save the planet. As he scrolls through the arguments raging on different platforms, the feeling of the injustice of the vote wells inside him. His team had been so close to history but the bureaucrats, in one fell swoop, had destroyed a lifetime of work and progress.

This could not possibly be the end: there would be retribution.

At 2:45 PM, a notification appears on his screen from his private messaging platform. It reads: "This is an urgent message regarding the Summit vote. Please do not ignore."

Next to the text is a link to a message.

Victor puts on his eXtended Reality headset and hits Play.

CHAPTER 2

"Greetings, Dr Bukowski. Please forgive me for using your private messaging channel to contact you."

Victor is sitting in a virtual room. Above him, a dome is covered with a map of the earth that is slowly rotating, emitting a soft, ambient light. The floor is pitch black. Opposite him is an olive-green wingback armchair supporting an avatar of a petite woman in a slate-blue business suit. Her hair is tied back into a ponytail, accentuating her delicate features.

She continues speaking. "As non-verified users, we had to work around the security protocols to message you, but the importance of what I have to say will justify our actions."

She blinks and looks down for a brief moment.

"My name is Ren Aoki, and I am speaking to you from Tokyo, Japan. This message is pre-recorded, so we will not be able to discuss anything. I will explain why when we meet. If we do."

Victor resists the urge to respond and concentrates on Ren's words, her Japanese accent diluted by American influence.

She continues. "I work for a private organisation whose single focus is the development of Artificial Intelligence for the benefit of humanity. We believe we have a duty to future generations to provide the tools they need not only to survive, but to thrive. Our current trajectory is one of imminent social, environmental, and economic destruction and this must be averted."

Her eyes narrow, then relax.

"As one of the foremost scientists in this field, you, too, see the importance of AI's further development as a safety net for our species. We have watched you with great admiration tirelessly campaign to stop the Shutdown. We listened to your speech at the AI Summit and were moved by your passion and reasoning. Like you, we were mortified by the 'Yes' vote which has brought about the Shutdown. We, too, believe that AI is the only way to change our species' terminal course and that stopping research and development in this field is humanity's gravest mistake."

Ren pauses, and Victor's avatar crosses his legs, motion signals picked up from the sensors on his XR headset. Ren's avatar, he guesses, is like his, an almost exact replica of her real self. His virtual character is distinguished by the same narrow brow and dark, deep-set features. He has the face of a boxer, it has been said, and the eyes of a preacher. His avatar is dressed in the default black suit, white shirt and thin black tie he is known for in real life, a *Men In Black*-style outfit.

"We need your help, Dr Bukowski. We have a Quantum AI Sandbox which, we believe, is on the cusp of Superintelligence: cognitive powers at an almost infinite scale."

The dome ceiling dissolves and the inside of a data centre materialises around them. They are now sitting in the middle of a space about half a football pitch in size with rows of steel cabinets the height of two refrigerators around it. A dozen steel desks and workstations are set up as an island in the middle.

Ren stands and points to one cabinet. Its cover disappears revealing the component parts of a Quantum computer shielded within. The central unit, a cylindrical tank, flies out into virtual space, and its casing vanishes, revealing the beautiful innards of a chandelier-like Quantum computer.

A charcoal-grey metal cylinder supports half a dozen gold plates the size of truck wheels with half-metre gaps connected by thousands of thin gold cables. Behind these, circuits, panels and intricate honeycomb structures glint and shine like alien jewels and decorations. A tiny microchip that would fit into the palm of a hand floats out of the bottom of the structure into the space between Victor and Ren.

"This is one of thirty Quantum computers in our facility," continues Ren. "One of the most powerful configurations of technology in the world. The processor in front of you has a capacity of over thirty million qubits. That, in total, is almost one billion qubits more than any other Quantum facility in the world. Enough power to realise our ambitions for Superintelligence."

The exposed computer returns to its cabinet. The laboratory disappears and they are again sitting under the dome.

Victor is still trying to assess whether this is an elaborate hoax. The most advanced Quantum facility he has worked on had a three-hundred-million-qubit capacity. A total of thirty with close to a billion qubits is simply unbelievable. What he could do with that power is beyond exciting.

"You must be wondering if this is real," says Ren, as if reading his mind. "The fact that you have never heard of our facility must make you distrust what I have just shown you. All I can do now is to assure you that it is real and offer you the opportunity to come and see it yourself. We anticipated this day, which is why this facility is hidden. It is imperative that it remain so."

She interlinks her hands, rests them on her lap and pauses. "What I am offering you, Victor, is an opportunity to build what you've dreamt of all your life. The risks are high and the penalties for being caught severe. However, you need to choose now what you will do. Your choice is to ignore this message and to carry on with your life, or to meet a driver at this location at 2 AM tomorrow."

A location appears on the screen. It's a side road near the Camden lock he knows well. The location vanishes and is replaced by a countdown clock. 11 hours, 8 minutes and 23 seconds until collection.

"If you choose to meet our driver, we will fly you to Tokyo

on a private jet. No one will know you have left your country. No one must know, or our plan will fail. This is of the utmost importance, Dr Bukowski. I realise this may seem like a crazy request, but our times demand unconventional actions. Please be sure that all this is real. To prove we are serious we have sent you something which will be arriving shortly."

Ren stands and bows.

"Goodbye. I hope to see you soon."

Ren and the virtual room disappear, leaving Victor in his Virtual Home Space, a perfect replica of the inside of the Sagrada Familia in Barcelona, Spain. He lifts his XR headset off, heart racing and begins to process Ren's message.

The doorbell chimes, jolting him out of thought.

Parcel Delivery.

Victor exits the flat to collect the package from the secure bin where delivery drones deposit goods. It is about the size of a paperback novel. Once back inside, he carefully removes the packaging and opens the cardboard box. His eyes narrow as he takes in what he is seeing: resting safely in a moulded impression is a Quantum chip. He takes it out and holds it up to the light between his thumb and index finger.

He has seen Quantum processors closely before, but this looks generations ahead of those. He rotates it and marvels at the beauty and intricacy of the design. This tiny piece of hardware would be worth many millions, if not more. But it was not the price that excited him, it was the possibilities that greater computational power could bring. This wasn't just a chip; this was a small building block of the future of humanity.

Whoever sent this, thinks Victor, means business.

The pressure to make a quick decision is tightening in his chest. He clenches and opens his fists repetitively, a coping mechanism he developed to deal with high-stress situations. Worst-case scenario, this could be a scam or a trap and he could end up in prison, throwing his life and career away. Actually, the worst-case scenario is that he could risk his life.

Part of him wishes he could forget the whole thing and

get some bloody sleep. Perhaps it's the lack of sleep, the jet lag, the frustration of seeing years of toil flushed down the toilet, but a voice deep inside him is screaming: "Go!"

He paces around his living room, weighing the decision in his mind.

The opportunity to work in a Quantum facility with that much power is an irresistible draw. The speed at which it could train his Neural Net with the vast amount of data he has collected and curated would be unparalleled. But what is most exciting is how it would be able to create simulations and synthetic data to retrain itself under its own guidance in near-real-time.

He stops in front of a picture on the wall. It depicts him and two other scientists receiving a Turing award for their work in Human-Machine Collaboration using Neural Links. His stomach lurches at the thought of the protests and threats from the AI doomsdayers that followed the winning the award.

The fear-based narrative spreads like wildfire: if computers could understand the human condition, they would use that knowledge to manipulate us and ultimately destroy us. They were wrong then as they are now, and this could be an opportunity to demonstrate the benign qualities of synthetic intelligence.

Victor knows that he will go whatever the consequence. Not trying would bear too high a price. The forever unquenched curiosity and passed opportunity would plague him for the rest of his days.

Now decided, he makes another coffee and drinks it slowly on the sofa, his crash pad between international adventures. He checks his bags from the recent inbound journey. He allows himself some time to rest. Not easily done against the rising tide of anxiety.

CHAPTER 3

At 1:30 AM, Victor leaves his flat and turns down the high street towards Chalk Farm. The night is uncharacteristically cold for early summer, around three degrees, and fog has descended providing beneficial conditions for cover. The weather reminds Victor of last year, at the beginning of summer, when a severe hailstorm blasted through London causing significant damage to buildings and cars. These anomalies were becoming more frequent and fuelling the doomsday fears of climate change.

He is wearing a black puffer jacket with a high collar and a flat cap firmly placed on his head. Hanging from his shoulders is a backpack. He is also carrying a cabin-sized suitcase which he doesn't want to drag noisily behind him along the pavement, as it may attract unwanted attention. The light stuttering from the occasional temperamental LED streetlamp accompanies him on his walk. The fog catches the bursts of light in its embrace before releasing it again into the darkness.

Most bars and restaurants are closed this early on a Monday morning. Street life consists of sketchy characters lurking in doorways, packs of young revellers heading home or wandering aimlessly, and strays floating around like ghosts, untethered and drifting along the streets with no apparent direction. The early morning quiet is amplified by the fog and infused with the purr of passing electric vehicle motors and the continuous hum of drones overhead along the skyways.

Victor's heart is pulsing and he senses he is being watched. He pulls the tip of his flat cap further down and quickens his pace. He continues up the main road past the shops with giant murals and installations decorating their walls. A twelve-foot spiderweb with neon strands glowing in a sequence of patterns casts pools of changing colours onto the shining streets.

Some of the facades combine physical art and holographic projections, making it often impossible to tell the difference between what is real and what is computer generated. The inner works of a giant grandfather clock are installed on the front of a famous local bookstore called The Midnight Library. The cogs in the installation spin and drive a complex set of pistons and pumps. The Steampunk aesthetic is popular in Camden.

Paranoia is unsettling Victor and dark figures appear in his outer field of vision, startling him, then passing by harmlessly. The main road is exposed to the all-seeing CCTV. There is no way for him to know if he is being watched or followed.

He reaches the Camden Lock, passes over the canal bridge, past the Banksy-inspired mural of Android Child Playing in a Sandpit, and into Chalk Farm Road. After a few hundred metres, he turns into Crossland Road, left then right, and eventually reaches the location given by Ren.

It's 1:45 AM. Fifteen minutes to pick-up.

Victor stands against the wall at the end of a terrace of Georgian houses. A nearby tree gives him some cover from overhead cameras, and from his vantage point he can see ingress and egress points into the designated spot. There are no cars or pedestrians around. He waits, watching intently, breathing slowly and deeply to calm his nerves.

This is his last chance to abandon the mission, he reflects. He will now plunge deeper into the unknown and soon be completely submerged.

A beam of light cuts through the fog, partially blinding

him. It's precisely 2:00 AM. His eyes adjust to observe a sleek black Sedan approach, slow down and come to a stop by the roadside. The inconspicuous car emits a soft click and ding, and the boot and rear passenger door open. It sits there like a panther waiting to seize its prey. Victor wills his body to move towards it. Overcoming his nerves, and holding his breath, he approaches the car, places his luggage in the boot and bundles himself into the rear passenger seat. The door closes automatically.

A black panel separates him from the driver's section. The car silently begins its journey onwards. In this leather-clad cave filled with silence and the smell of valeting, the reality of his situation hits him like a wave. His journey has begun. Perhaps it is a catastrophic error of judgement. Following a sudden urge, he knocks on the black panel separating him from the driver.

Nothing.

CHAPTER 4

The car glides through the fog-shrouded streets as if through a dream. Victor watches the ghostly shapes of buildings and vehicles pass by, taking him through a world both familiar and alien.

The voice of a chauffeur with a warm English accent fills the car. "Dr Bukowski, my name is CATE, and I am your Automated Driving Assistant." He had hoped for a human driver rather than an AI.

"Please relax," continues CATE, "This journey will take approximately three hours. You will find refreshments to your left."

Victor glances over to a tray filled with an assortment of food and drink: water, Diet Coke, crisps, sandwiches and nuts, each tucked into its own mini compartment. He reaches for the water and takes a sip, contemplating his situation.

"Where are we going?"

"We are travelling to a private airfield where you will board your flight to Tokyo," CATE replies.

"I'm assuming I won't be going through passport control?"

"No. Your departure must be kept a secret."

Victor leans back in his seat, digesting this information. "I'm being smuggled?"

"Yes, you could say that," CATE replies, her tone neutral.

Victor's mind races. "I walked along a high street to

get here. I've probably been picked up by a dozen CCTV feeds already."

"All evidence of your walking here has been erased," CATE reassures him.

"What about my geolocation? I've probably broadcast my location to a dozen satellites or cellular towers."

"Our Operatives are experts in concealing digital trails."

Something isn't adding up. "Why not pick me up outside my flat?"

CATE confirms his thinking: "We had to monitor you to see if you were being followed."

"Who would be following me?"

"I'm sorry, I don't have an answer to that question."

"Excuse me?"

"I'm sorry, I don't have an answer to that question."

Victor sighs, reminding himself he is talking to a program.

"What does CATE stand for?" he asks, fully aware that most autonomous assistant names are acronyms.

"Charming Autonomous Transport Experience."

Victor smirks. "You're meant to be charming?"

"Yes, to provide comfort in what is most likely an anxiety-inducing situation."

"Who do you work for?"

"I'm sorry, I don't have an answer to that question."

Victor falls silent, resigned. These conversation bots are typical of today's synthetic intelligence: uncanny replications of humanity with eerily authentic speech patterns and understanding of emotion and intent. But this veil of human behaviour can always be lifted to reveal the true nature of these machines. Human taught, human controlled, incapable of creative thinking.

"How are you feeling, Dr Bukowski?" asks CATE after a long pause. "Would you like the temperature adjusted?

"I'm not great, CATE. I'd like more information about who you work for. That would make me feel better."

"I'm sorry, Dr Bukowski. My programming doesn't allow me to engage in conversation relating to your assignment. We can discuss anything else, if you wish," she responds, sounding apologetic.

"Can you tell me where this private airfield is we are going to?"

"The less you know, Dr Bukowski, the better," CATE answers.

Victor swipes his wrist to activate his Retinal Display. Nothing happens.

"I must apologise, Victor. Personal Systems access is prohibited and blocked inside this vehicle. You cannot use your Cube, Retinal Displays, XR Glasses, or any other peripheral device."

"Charming indeed..."

The headlights of another car suddenly flood the cabin of the vehicle with light and Victor turns to look through the back window. A Tesla behind is following closely.

His heart begins to pound against his chest.

"Do not worry, that vehicle is registered to a civilian who is not a threat. It will pass soon."

As predicted, the Tesla behind overtakes them.

Victor takes a sharp in-breath: "Someone in a rush, I guess."

"Would you like relaxing music? I can access your listening history and curate a most pleasurable playlist."

"That is my private data, CATE!"

"Our operatives are experts in...."

"Never mind," he interrupts. "Sure, CATE. You find something good."

The melodic rhythms of Miles Davis resume and he closes his eyes, trying to dilute the adrenaline coursing through his body and to calm his whirling mind.

CHAPTER 5

The journey takes Victor into the remote English countryside, the car snaking along narrow winding roads. With no maps or geolocation information and the outside world bathed in darkness, he is utterly lost. As the three-hour journey time approaches, the Sedan leaves the main road, and a sequence of intermittent stops and starts hints at their impending arrival.

Finally, around what he estimates to be around 5 A.M., the vehicle pulls to a stop, and CATE says: "You have arrived at your destination. Thank you for your company, Dr Bukowski. I wish you well on your journey." The passenger door opens, allowing a blast of fresh chilly air into the vehicle. He is greeted by a tall and thin, dark-skinned man wearing a heavy coat, protective face mask and pilot's cap.

"Dr Bukowski, please follow me," the man commands with a strong Egyptian accent, his voice gruff and impatient. With an unsettled feeling, Victor follows him to a sleek private jet. It is poised on an empty runway, an ethereal strip of asphalt illuminated inside the fog by yellow lights on its edges and stretching into the darkness.

Victor follows the man up the flight of stairs into the aircraft.

The smell of leather hits Victor as he enters the spacious and luxurious interior. There is a cream armchair and table, a small kitchenette, and a three-seater sofa settled at the far end of the cabin. The walls and ceiling are made of Digi-Fabric, displaying various soothing, ambient scenes. Currently, an abstract world map paints the interior in an electric azure blue. It reminds Victor of his virtual meeting with Ren.

"Take a seat, Dr Bukowski, and fasten your seatbelt. We will be departing shortly. I will let you know when you are free to move around. You can then help yourself to food and drink."

The pilot bows, seals the cabin and enters the cockpit through a discreet panel which Victor had not noticed until now.

In under ten minutes, the hum of the jet engine turns into a mighty roar, and it leaps into the skies. The swiftness of departure is an unsettling reminder that his hosts have a genuine fear of him being followed.

Once in the air, the pilot informs him he is free to move, and he unstraps his seat belt and goes to the kitchenette. On the counter is a tray with a platter of freshly made sushi arranged in meticulous rows. Adrenaline is still in his system, muting his appetite. He places a few pieces onto a plate, pours himself a glass of fine Scottish whisky and sits down on the sofa and begins to eat. The delicate scent of fresh fish and fragrant rice stir his hunger and he savours the intricate tastes and textures of each bite.

After this interlude, Victor stretches out on the sofa and lets his mind drift. The medicinal punch of the whisky lingers on his tongue and opens him up to the fatigue which has been waiting to take hold. He feels its tendrils twisting deep into his body and wrapping themselves around his mind, pulling it into oblivion. He falls into a disturbed sleep, his adrenaline still upsetting the fragile separation between his consciousness and his unconscious.

In the theatre of his mind, his dreams play out, and in his fitful state, the images, emotions and stories leave detailed imprints in his memory: the autonomous street cleaner features, clumsily crashing into cars parked along the road and wielding its mechanical limbs like weapons.

There are prisons, too, from which he tries to escape,

getting lost in a labyrinth of dead-end corridors lined with cells where faceless prisoners stare at him blankly, not revealing any emotion: no anger, no desperation.

And then there are algorithms, manifested as impossibly complex Rubik's cube-like structures and a choking feeling of hopelessness trying to solve them.

Victor wakes up and checks the clock on a nearby display. He has been asleep for just over eight hours. He heads off to the shower facilities, peels off his clothes, steps into the cubicle and twists the dial. The hum of the plane engines dissolves into the sound of the shower jet. Standing under the cascade of water, Victor lets it wash away his mental debris and clear his mind.

Dressed and ready, Victor returns to his seat. An announcement soon comes and the pilot requests to get ready for landing. Victor's stomach knots as he prepares for the next leg of his adventure: meeting Ren Aoki.

Hoping they are landing in Japan, Victor remembers his first visit to Tokyo two years ago, to speak at an AI conference on the ethics of creating simulated consciousness. It was about the same time of year as now, early summer, with binding heat and humidity that would cling to you like a second skin, and heavy thunderstorms that would blast through the city, increasing further the level of humidity.

There, he had his first taste of real sushi in a small shack on Tsukiji Fish Market. He had to queue and when his turn came, he sat down and ate silently and without delay. The feeling of the delicate slices of fresh mango and creamy uni melting in his mouth, combined with the sharp tang of the wasabi and the earthiness of the soy sauce, was an explosion of perfectly harmonised flavours which he had never experienced before.

Vivid recollections of walking through the serene and majestic Yoyogi park flash through his mind, the whispers of the towering trees, the melancholy cawing of its large crow population, and the calming rhythm of the water cleansing station in front of Meiji Shrine, a momentary sanctuary from the vibrant energy of the city. Not far away, the Akihabara's

Electric Town pulsed with light creating an incessant cacophony of electronic sounds.

During the conference, Victor had met an elderly Japanese professor. Despite the language barrier, they spent an evening exchanging ideas through a younger colleague who spoke good English, drawn together by their shared interest in AI ethics. The professor had invited Victor to a traditional Japanese tea ceremony and he had been deeply moved by the grace, patience, and mindfulness present in every action of the host. This experience, too, had left an indelible mark, reminding him of the importance of considering the human element in the advance of technology.

As the jet descends, Victor looks at the sealed window preventing him from seeing outside. His anxiety returns, his mind reeling with different possibilities of where they were actually landing and who would be there to meet him.

The aircraft hits the tarmac with a barely perceptible jolt and the brakes are applied, forcing his body against the resistance of the seatbelt. It comes to a stop and the engine shuts off. An oppressive silence follows. The door will open soon and reveal his destination. Adrenaline fires up his heart and heightens his senses.

Another pilot, a slight Japanese man, who he hadn't seen throughout the journey, emerges from the cabin and bows.

"Dr Bukowski, we have arrived. You are now at a private airfield outside greater Tokyo."

"Good news," mutters Victor.

The pilot opens the reinforced cabin door and Victor's eyes adjust to the darkness outside. It is nighttime, which is a comforting. His doubts regarding where he was landing are further dispelled as the local time would be around midnight in Tokyo. He looks down the stairs. A man and a woman are approaching from the edge of the illuminated runway. A black saloon is parked nearby. He immediately recognises Ren Aoki marching purposefully towards the jet.

When he sets foot on the asphalt, she bows and says

with a warm smile: "Welcome to Japan, Dr Bukowski. We are so grateful for you to be here." She is wearing a black light jacket, the fabric decorated with intricate embroidery of wave patterns. Her hair is styled in an elegant bun at the back of her head.

Victor returns the bow, a custom he has always enjoyed. "Thank you, Miss Aoki. It is a pleasure to be back."

"We have a car waiting, Dr Bukowski. Come with us." There is a hint of urgency and nervousness in her voice.

The man next to her, a man in his early thirties dressed in plain grey suit with a square face and a scar running along his jaw, collects Victor's bag, and they head to the nearby vehicle. The air is humid and the scent of a summer thunderstorm lingers.

Victor climbs in and sits opposite Ren in the back of the vehicle while the escort takes the front. He places on his XR headset and the car begins to move, navigating towards its destination.

Ren leans forwards a fraction. "Thank you again for making the trip, Dr Bukowski. We can't express our gratitude enough."

"Can you tell me who 'we' is?"

"I'm sorry, Doctor. This is a difficult question to answer now. More will be revealed over time. The Shutdown has made secrecy key to our survival. I can tell you that 'we' are many people belonging to an organisation called Miyamoto."

"Miyamoto, as in Miyamoto Musashi, the famous swordsman?"

"Yes, you know Japanese history well. Miyamoto Musashi was a great warrior and military strategist. He was the catalyst behind the reunification of warring Japan."

"You believe your Miyamoto will bring about unification in Japan?"

"Beyond that, Doctor. Unification across the divided world. Only unification can alter our trajectory as a species. Divided, we will fall."

"And your work in AI is the key? The warrior that can

bring harmony and heal our planet?"

Ren nods and examines Victor, scrutinising his face for a response.

"Nice name." Outside, a steady flow of cars and lorries stream past with shadowed figures ensconced in their digital bubbles ignoring the world around them. Ren remains silent.

"Can you tell me who I will be working with? Or where I'll be working?"

"I will be your only direct contact. And Haruto, my colleague in the front. Many others are involved in running our facility - hardware and software engineers, analysts, system architects and administrators, to name a few - but they will be operating behind the scenes. You will never meet them nor learn their names or identities."

"Are you the head of Miyamoto?"

"No. The Sponsor is the chief financier and strategist. I run the operations of the facility."

"I don't suppose you can tell me who the Sponsor is?"

Ren dips her head apologetically. "I am sorry, no."

"The Sponsor is the money behind Miyamoto?"

"More than money, Doctor. Much more."

Ren's expression stiffens, hinting that this line of questioning is at a dead end. Victor changes tack.

"I apologise for the barrage of questions but I'm sure you can appreciate it is important for me to know what I am potentially getting myself into."

"Of course, Doctor. Please ask anything you wish, but you must appreciate that secrecy is critical now."

"I would like to know more about where I will be working. Will it be at the Quantum facility you showed me? How do we access it?"

"You will be working at the Quantum facility you saw. Access is highly secured."

"And it's actually a Sandbox?"

"Yes, it is completely cut off from the outside world and the only way to access its resources is to be physically present inside the facility." Ren continues. "The facility is located deep underground, in a warehouse created as part of the Tokyo Metro development. There are a few of these warehouses, some known and others not. You will be working near an unnamed station on the Oedo line, Tokyo's deepest subway. I am the gatekeeper to the facility."

"That must have been a near-impossible task - building one of the largest Quantum facilities in the world in a secret underground warehouse. Who else knows about this warehouse?"

"The location of the warehouse is only known by The Sponsor, me, Haruto and a few trusted members. And yes, the project was a challenge, but we believe in making the impossible possible. That is what we are trying to achieve."

"Others must know of the facility. That it exists."

"Yes, scientists and engineers who belong to Miyamoto know it exists and work on it. The exact location and access, however, is hidden from them."

"What about the workers who built it?"

"They were transported in and out of the facility through a series of gated control points, making access impossible without my knowledge. They would spend months working on site, and materials and equipment were transported through a network of tunnels. We would replace the assembly teams at regular intervals to ensure no one could become too familiar with our operation. It was a challenge to build the facility in component parts while keeping a large workforce ignorant to our plans. But with the right planning, coordination and orchestration, you would be amazed what we can do."

"Impressive," Victor acknowledges. "I would like to know more about your AI. You said that you were close to a breakthrough?"

A ping from Ren's watch interrupts their dialogue.

"I must take this call. I will give you more details if you agree to help us." Ren places her hands on her lap, clasping her fingers together. "Before I take this call, Doctor, there is something important I must tell you."

Nerves flutter through Victor's stomach.

Ren breathes in deeply and continues. "Until you agree to work with us, you are free to return home and we will never speak again. However, if you sign up with Miyamoto, you will be under strict terms of confidentiality. The consequences you face if you break this confidentially will be severe. We have all agreed to these terms but not many are willing to...." Ren stops, deciding she has said enough.

"And these terms... and penalties are?" Victor asks, not masking his alarm.

"They will be presented to you at the right time. As I say, Doctor, at any point, you are free to return home." A sternness comes over Ren. "We will compensate you handsomely for your time with us and you will never see or hear from us again. If you are still interested in continuing the journey with us, then be patient. We will give you enough information to make the right decision. Now, I must take this call."

Ren opens a small drawer below her seat, pulls out an XR headset, and places it on her head. She swipes the air several times and then begins a conversation in Japanese with her virtual caller.

Meanwhile, questions race through Victor's mind. Who is the Sponsor? Is this Quantum facility as advanced as promised? How on earth did they build it and keep it secret from the public, from the government? And what were the penalties she referred to?

Just what in God's name is he getting himself to?

CHAPTER 6

The car journey ends at Tokyo's Midtown, one of the many cities within the metropolis. Ren informs him he will be called upon in a few days. She explains there is an unavoidable delay. Victor's doubts and worries mount but he decides to follow along until he has enough information to decide what to do. She wishes him a good rest and he steps out of the vehicle.

He is ushered by the escort into an innocuous block of flats just off Hinokicho Park, a tranquil landscaped garden with a small lake; it is a quiet oasis in the high-density, high-tech spectacle of many other districts. They enter an empty foyer and the man summons the lift. With a strong accent, he introduces himself as Haruto. He has a good command of English, and a clipped precise delivery.

They arrive at the sixth floor, enter the genkan of one of three apartments. In this small entryway, they remove their shoes before stepping onto the wooden flooring of the living space. One side of the room is lined with large cupboards with sliding doors covered with paper. The living room has a cream sofa with grey cotton cushions. There is a low square polished wooden table with large slim sitting cushions arranged around it. On the far end is the kitchen. In a small adjacent room a workstation and a desk and chair are set up. Two sliding shoji doors made of thick rice paper over wooden frames separate the living room from what must be a bedroom. Other doors lead to the bathroom and a separate toilet. The walls are blank.

"Welcome to your apartment, Dr Bukowski," says Haruto, placing Victor's bags on the floor. "This building is owned by a subsidiary of Miyamoto - untraceable back to the organisation, of course. There are only a handful of other residents. In any case, Japanese culture, as you may know, dictates that people living in flats should be mindful of their neighbours, so it should be quiet and you will be undisturbed. Over there is your workstation." He points to the glass table and chair which suddenly appears to Victor incredibly alien next to the traditional Japanese interior.

"Will I be able to access the Ether?"

"Yes, your access to the Ether is re-instated while you are here. But please be aware that everything you do will be monitored as we cannot allow you to make contact with anyone in the outside world. We will manage your online activity which will give the impression you are travelling and taking some time out after the Summit."

"And if I want to leave the apartment?"

"We cannot allow this."

"No sightseeing, then."

Haruto doesn't smile. "Dr Bukowski, you have been smuggled to Tokyo and are working for an organisation that is developing technology that is now illegal. I'm sure you won't be surprised at the stringent measures we need to take to ensure your presence is kept a secret. You will not leave this apartment. Although you can access the Ether, you will under no circumstances communicate with anyone. If you do, Miyamoto will know and your assignment will cease immediately."

"And what happens if the assignment ceases?"

"You will be transported back to your home and all traces of our relationship will be erased. I hope I have made myself clear, Dr Bukowski."

"I need to speak to my daughter, Haruto. This is a non-negotiable."

Haruto pauses briefly and then replies, as if expecting

this request. "We will allow you to speak to your daughter once, Dr Bukowski. We will be monitoring your call and you will not give any information regarding where you are. After that, all outside communications will cease unless authorised. That is our non-negotiable."

Victor nods in agreement.

"Now if there is anything you need, please let me know and I will do my best to accommodate your request. I have sent the details of my private communication channel to you."

With this, Haruto bows and leaves. Victor remains standing, taking in the details of his elegant prison.

A sudden pang of claustrophobia tightens his chest. He lets it pass and focuses on what he can do in this environment. He will explore how he can push his Neural Net architecture to take advantage of the Quantum computing power of the facility. He isn't sure how sophisticated the Miyamoto AI Systems are but has yet to see anything to rival his work in areas beyond the latest technology in Artificial General Intelligence, or AGI.

Unlocking these capabilities is the key to achieving AGI, intelligence that goes beyond the capability to classify, predict, or act on a set of inputs. This will be an intelligence that recognises, recollects, and reasons. These dimensions of intelligence are the most elusive to the engineers of simulated human intellect, and Victor believes he is one of the few scientists close to attaining them. All that stands in his way is enough power to bring them to life; power now apparently within his grasp. And if Miyamoto is close to cracking this cerebral code, he simply has to see it for himself.

The first thing Victor decides to do is to call his daughter.

He sits down on one of the floor cushions and places his Cube on the coffee table in front of him. "Call Natasha," he commands. A screen appears above the device with a static photo of his daughter. She is sitting on a giant bean bag, smiling broadly and looking away from the camera - intelligence, vitality and humour radiating from her in this candid moment. This is her at her best.

Natasha answers his video call after a few rings. She appears on his screen in her kitchen, groggy, golden hair tousled and unwieldy and making a late lunch. She looks thinner than when they last spoke, which spikes his paternal concern. After dropping out of her first year at university due to anxiety and depression, she is now supporting herself by waitressing at a Mexican restaurant in the West End of London.

"Hi, Dad!"

"Morning, Tash, glad I caught you before your evening shift."

The clanging of pots and pans can be heard in the background. "Just washing up and making food. Sorry about the racket."

Victor waits for a quiet moment before speaking. "We haven't spoken in a while and I wanted to see how you were."

"Surviving, Dad. I'm OK. What about you? I saw the news about the Summit in Geneva. I'm sorry about the vote, I know how hard you worked to stop it. Your speech was really brilliant! I can't imagine how painful it is to have your life's work stopped in its tracks by a bunch of bureaucrats. I'm sorry I didn't message but work has been crazy and I'm adjusting to life post Uni."

The drone-cam follows Natasha to the lounge where she is taking a bowl of pasta and sits at a small dining table. She has a video filter on but Victor can see dark shades under her eyes.

"The Summit's outcome was a difficult moment, but it's not over. I haven't given up hope."

Natasha gives a comforting smile. "I'd expect nothing less, Dad. You aren't going to dive, are you? Or go high?"

"No, Tash," a hint of defensiveness. "You know I haven't had a manic or depressive episode in years."

"I don't know, Dad. I haven't seen you in ages."

Victor stalls, not knowing how to respond. Depression, anxiety and mania were all traits of his bloodline and had taken their toll on him and generations before him, and, he believed, Natasha also carried this curse. He managed his manic depression through medication and a fanatical dedication to work. The latter got in the way of him being a good father and husband.

"What about you, Tash? I'm worried about you. I know things have been tough and I want to make sure I give you all the support you need."

A long pause ensues while Natasha considers her response. He guesses what she is thinking that he isn't there now and hasn't been countless times before. Guilt burns in his chest.

"I'm coping, Dad. You don't need to worry. Work is keeping me busy and I don't have much time to think of or feel anything else."

"Are you taking your meds?" He cringes as he helplessly watches himself take the conversation to this known trigger. But he has to ask. He has to know.

"Jesus Christ." Natasha puts down her spoon into the bowl and looks severely at the drone-cam hovering silently in front of her. The image of her father is projected above the cam. "Why do you always have to ask that? Can't you trust me to do the right thing for myself?"

"I know what you are going through, Tash," Victor pleads. "I've been there before. I'm asking because I care and I know medication will help."

"I'm not you, Dad. And I'm not one of your projects. As much as you think you can create the perfect human mind in a computer, you can't do that with me. I'm human, flawed, emotional, affected by my environment and my past. These are the sources of my pain, not a malfunction in my programming. I don't need a patch or an update or bloody medication."

"It's not just me," parries Victor. "Your mother would have wanted the same."

"Don't bring Mum into this Dad, please. You aren't in a position to speak for her." Natasha's voice starts to waver with emotion. "If you had been there more, when she was well, when she was sick, then..." She trails off.

Victor stops himself. He can hear the pain in Natasha's

voice. She was right, although he had tried to support her mother, Cassandra, from the day of her diagnosis through a devastating decline over six months, he still worked. A lot. He had constructed his own truth, his own reality, about how much he was there, how much support he gave. Since Cassandra's tragic death five years before, he had come to realise that truth was an invention, an unhealthy hallucination.

Victor sees he has to back off. These arguments always ended up with both of them more convinced they're right and deepen the ragged ravine between them.

"Sorry, Tash. I don't want to upset you. You know it's just because I love you and care. Since your mother died, I've tried my best to give you the support she provided you with. But I know I'm not present enough, and when I am, I'm going about it all wrong."

"I know you're trying your best, Dad. But I just need you to trust me." Natasha gives a weak smile and returns to her pasta. "Where are you, by the way?"

"Abroad."

Natasha is used to his random whereabouts and doesn't enquire further.

"I'm not sure how long I'm going to be away, Tash. But if you need me, I'll come home immediately."

"Thanks. We talking days, weeks, months?"

"I'm not sure yet."

"Do what you need to do, Dad." Then wearily: "I know you're trying to save the world..."

"Tash, please. You are so much more important to me than my work," Victor interjects.

Natasha snorts derisively then takes a deep breath. "Please don't feel guilty about being away. I'm a big girl and I have this under control. Sorry, Dad, I really need to go get ready for my shift." Natasha looks down. "This job is only temporary, I promise."

"Of course..." Victor stutters but Natasha stands and blows a kiss into the camera before disconnecting. Over and out.

Typically, Victor is left feeling hollow, guilty and helpless. If only her mother were still alive. She had supported Natasha through her childhood and early teens while he was an absent, workaholic father. When she had died, their worlds had been shaken to their core. Victor had tried to spend more time with Natasha, but his work was a powerful addiction that he seemed unable to break.

Even with the advances in medical treatment there was nothing that could be done for her. Many believed the fragile threads of life are sometimes destined to snap, leaving microscopic tears in rich tapestry of human existence, and deep gouges in the lives of the loved left behind. Victor believed if the technology had been more advanced, something could have been done to keep his beloved wife alive.

As usual, he goes for the easy option and pushes these lamentations to the back of his mind to refocus on his work. He turns off his Cube and places his XR headset on. The outside world fades away and his Hub materialises, wrapping around him an array of screens filled with dashboards, code, data and logs - the precious jewels he covets, and which take away his pain.

With a light swish of his finger, a carousel of screens revolves in front of him and he selects the latest version of his Neural Net. His software is running in his private cloud, hidden away from the prying eyes of those behind the Shutdown. The power of his servers is a tiny fraction of what the Quantum facility would offer but there is still work he can do to optimise the algorithms and harness the potential of hundreds of millions of qubits. The electric sensation of seemingly divine focus consumes Victor as he takes the next step on this journey. He needs this to help heal this broken world.

And nothing or nobody would stop him.

PART 2

Charles Kane

THREE MONTHS LATER

I am putting myself to the fullest possible use, which is all I think that any conscious entity can ever hope to do.

— HAL 9000, 2001: A SPACE ODYSSEY (1968)

You will be required to do wrong no matter where you go. It is the basic condition of life, to be required to violate your own identity. At some time, every creature which lives must do so. It is the ultimate shadow, the defeat of creation; this is the curse at work, the curse that feeds on all life. Everywhere in the universe.

— DO ANDROIDS DREAM OF ELECTRIC SHEEP?, PHILIP K. DICK (1968)

Cyberspace. A consensual hallucination experienced daily by billions of legitimate operators, in every nation, by children being taught mathematical concepts... A graphic representation of data abstracted from banks of every computer in the human system. Unthinkable complexity. Lines of light ranged in the nonspace of the mind, clusters and constellations of data. Like city lights, receding...

— William Gibson, Neuromancer

CHAPTER 7

"They're ready for you now, Mr Kane." A woman in her twenties smiles at the man sitting on a wooden armchair. Her pristine, professional appearance is at odds with the faded wallpaper of the small sitting room in which the grizzled detective is lethargically reclining in his seat."

"Not your fault, I know, but they sure like to keep people waiting, don't they?" Kane stands, revealing his six-foot-four frame as he does so. He irons out his paisley shirt with his hands and adjusts his black leather jacket. They walk silently along a few corridors to reach a beige door with a silver plaque reading Operations Room. The young woman opens the door and, with a fixed grin, gestures for him to enter.

The room is an office boardroom with a rectangular oak table around which are arranged a dozen leather chairs. It smells of furniture polish and stationery. Three of the chairs are occupied by two men and a woman looking at him expectantly. The middle suit, a man in his late fifties with slicked back blonde hair, greying at the sides, and a salt and pepper short beard, stands up.

"Mr Kane. A pleasure. Please take a seat." He points to the chair opposite him.

"Thank you for coming at such short notice," he continues. Kane folds himself down into the chair. "Your reputation precedes you and we have been very excited to meet you in person. My name is Jacob Peterson, and these are my colleagues, Andrea and Stephan."

"You all from NEST?" Kane asks as Peterson sits back down.

"Yes."

A short silence follows while Peterson waits for follow-up questions, but none come. "How much do you know about NEST?" he asks.

"NEST stands for..." Kane raises his index finger to allow him time to recall, "the international Network for the Enforcement of Synthetic inTelligence. You're the AI police."

"We wouldn't describe ourselves as 'police', but I can see how you might think that." Peterson shifts in his seat and leans forwards, forearms resting on the table. "Mr Kane, tell me what you know about the Shutdown."

"Christ, I didn't expect an interrogation," rebuts Kane. Peterson smiles, but his eyes remain cold, humourless.

"Bear with us, Mr Kane. It's important for us to understand how much you know, to set a baseline for this conversation."

Kane clears his throat and looks up. "Let's see... The Shutdown." Fingers drum on the table. "About three months ago, the United Nations council voted to stop any research and development into AI. Everyone voted to flip the switch. Kill the Hal. It pissed a lot of people off who believe AI isn't the bad guy it's depicted to be; that it's the key to survival, not the Terminator plotline being peddled in the mainstream media."

"And you're aware of the Mandate in place following the Shutdown?"

"Find another job if you're trying to build a computer brain."

Peterson shakes his head. "It's much more serious than just finding a new job, Mr Kane. Those who don't stop will be tried for crimes against humanity. The penalty for continued research into General AI is severe."

"That seems extreme," remarks Kane. "Severe punishment for scientific exploration?"

A flash of anger in Peterson's eyes. "Rise up, Judge of the earth; pay back to the proud what they deserve. Psalms 94:1-1. Pride is a sin, Mr Kane. And thinking we can create life is the most egregious form of pride there is."

"A first testament, guy, eh! Right, so you're not dicking around. I got that from the news coverage. Must be a challenge, asking the smartest minds in the world to give up their life's work?"

Peterson leans back in his chair, folding his hands on his lap. "Many disagree with the vote and will likely try to defy the Mandate and continue with their research. It is a global imperative that these detractors are found and stopped. Our intelligence suggests that the scientific community is on the cusp of realising Superintelligence and the consequences would be catastrophic if this was achieved."

"Pandora's Box."

"Exactly. Releasing true machine intelligence into the world will unleash a power we will not be able to contain. This will result in the demise of humankind, and we will be unable to stop it."

"You're worried computers will figure out we're the real threat to this planet and stamp us out like a colony of ants."

Peterson's expression stays neutral. "We do not hold the view that our species is doomed, and our primary objective is to prevent that from happening, by any means necessary."

"What about the countries who haven't signed up to the Mandate? How are you going to stop them from opening the box?"

"After the Shutdown vote, the Mandate was signed by all but five countries: India, North Korea, Egypt, Syria, and Libya. We have deep-cover agents working in those territories to monitor scientific progress. Our intelligence suggests they are not currently a threat."

"And for the ones that are, how do you plan to beat the smartest people on the planet?"

Peterson scoffs. "We have the full support of the

international military and security organisations working with us. There are some pretty smart people there too."

"Good for you! With the world's brains and military might at your disposal, why do you need me?"

"In a word: Japan. And specifically your knowledge and experience of Tokyo."

Kane winces. "Those days are long behind me. I haven't been to Japan in almost ten years. And besides, who would want to go to Tokyo in August? You ever experienced the humidity in late summer?"

"Mr Kane," Peterson intercepts, "you spent the better part of your career working in Tokyo's darkest quarters. Your knowledge of and connections to the hidden part of Japan is second to none. It is this knowledge we need to help us."

"Help you with what exactly?" Kane leans forwards and rests his forearms on the table, mirroring Peterson's posture.

Peterson reclines slightly, clears his throat and pauses. "Would you like a drink, Mr Kane?"

"Call me Charles. And no, thanks, I'm fine."

Peterson stands, walks to a small table set against the far wall and pours himself a glass of water. His back is turned to Kane, leaving him in an uncomfortable stare with the two other suits.

"You two don't say much," he observes.

The woman doesn't react but the man retorts calmly: "We're here to listen and observe, Mr Kane."

Peterson returns to his chair and takes a sip of water.

"Mr Kane," he smiles, again with no warmth, "our interest in Tokyo is based on intelligence regarding a powerful Sandbox in the city."

"A Sandbox?"

"A Sandbox is a computer facility sealed off from the outside world. Before the Shutdown, Sandboxes were permitted facilities where cutting-edge AI could be developed.

Only a handful of known Sandboxes had enough computing power to bring about true machine intelligence."

Kane furrows his brow. "By 'sealed off from the world', you mean like on a volcanic island, or something?"

"No, we mean cut off from the Ether or any external networks. If a Superintelligence had access to the outside world, we wouldn't be able to control it and that's when it becomes an existential threat."

Kane rubs his eyes, sweeps back his salt-grey fringe and reclines in his seat. "Artificial Intelligence, super or not so super, isn't really my forte. You've got the wrong guy for the job."

Firmly, "Mr Kane..."

"Charles."

"Mr Kane, we aren't trying to hire you for your technical expertise, we are trying to hire you because you are an exceptional detective and have exactly the experience we need to track down a Sandbox which, we believe, is hidden somewhere in Tokyo."

"Don't you have any local talent in Japan? I am a Gaijin who sticks out like a sore thumb."

Peterson sighs. "You are not a Gaijin anymore, Mr Kane. You were once when you graduated there in journalism and became one of the few westerners to work at the highest levels at the Yomiuri Shimbun media corporation. But when you were later adopted by the Yakuza as their investigative reporter-cum-detective, you transcended your status and became elite in the social ranks of Japanese society."

"Don't you believe it, Mr Peterson. The non-Japanese never stop being Gaijin in Japan. It is most perilous to believe otherwise."

Silence fills the room, then Peterson continues. "We do have people on the inside... but so far, they have not been able to find the Sandbox."

"You think the Yakuza have something to do with this?" asks Kane.

"We hypothesise it is being funded by the Yakuza or a cell within the organisation. That is why you were recommended."

"You know I served three years for my... work with them.

You think I want to go back inside?"

Peterson shakes his head. "You will be working for the government, Mr Kane, well, many governments, to be precise. You will have full immunity no matter how unconventional your methods are."

A long silence ensues. Besides the potential dangers of this assignment, Kane remembers his old enemies with scores to settle. Brutal, ruthless enemies. "Sorry, I've got enough work on, and this assignment would be a death sentence. You're going to have to find someone else."

"We're sorry you feel that way, Mr Kane. But you haven't heard our offer yet. Stephan?"

The Suit slides a folded piece of paper across the table. Kane picks it up, slowly unfolds it and begins reading the contents.

"Shutting down this Sandbox is pretty important to you, eh?" He places the paper back on the table and looks at Peterson.

"More than you could know, Mr Kane."

A powerful urge rises within Kane, one he is all too familiar with. He recognises it and succumbs to it, as he had done countless times in the past.

"Well, that is, as they say, an offer I can't refuse. When do I start?"

CHAPTER 8

Annike De Ruiter lies on a bright orange upholstered armchair with reclining back and footrest, immersed in a virtual world. She is wearing a black tank top, cargo trousers and a hoodie and looks to be in her mid- to late twenties.

"Mr Kane! Give me a minute; just wrapping something up," she announces as Kane nears. She has an accent, probably Dutch.

"Call me Charles," he replies and waits for Annike to re-enter reality.

It's the following day and he is standing in a cavernous room in the basement of a council block of flats in Peckham, South London. The room is dim and primarily illuminated by strip lighting in chevron formations along the walls. There are no windows, and it could be the middle of the night as opposed to late afternoon. The air is damp and chilly, with a chalky, musky scent.

There are about four semi-separated sections in the room, each with one or two chairs like the one Annike is sitting on, coffee tables and standard armchairs, and divided from the other sections with noble, freestanding bookshelves. The cement floors are laid with a mosaic of rugs, many Persian, frayed, with corners curling up like fists.

A long, narrow metal table runs through the middle of the room like a spine connecting the spaces. The table is littered with broken electronics, half-finished circuits, and glowing devices that look on the cusp of life or death. About a dozen people are distributed around the basement in similar modes to Annike.

Eventually, she removes her headset and chimes, "Call me Anni", climbs off her chair, and approaches while fixing her shoulder-length, white-dyed hair into a ponytail. She stops at arm's length distance from Kane and pushes her hands in her pockets. "Fancy a cuppa... Charles?"

"Coffee, if you have?"

"We're out of milk. Black OK?"

Kane nods, and Annike takes two mugs from a nearby table and shares the contents of a percolated coffee pot between them.

"Have a seat," she points at two brown leather armchairs positioned around a steel coffee table.

Annike places the mugs on the table and sits down.

"Any trouble finding me?" she asks.

"No, a young chap with tattoos led me to you. He had a strange hat on." Kane cranes his neck to look behind him and see if he can point him out. He has vanished.

Annike smiles. "That must be Xavier. He loves his headgear."

Kane clears his throat. "Thank you for taking the time to see me, Annike. NEST said you are one of the best trackers around. And when it comes to AI, you know about everyone in the game."

Annike doesn't react.

"I'm sure you've got better things to do?" he finishes and glances over at her virtual station.

"It's fine. They're paying me. You have my undivided attention. Tell me what you want to know." She locks her gaze onto Kane with a fierce intensity.

"Right," says Kane, sorting through his thoughts to find a good lead-in question. "Uhhh..."

"They said you are pretty new to this world," Annike cuts in. "Let me help."

"That would be great."

"You're looking for a Sandbox hidden in Tokyo, right?"

Kane nods.

"You're familiar with what a Sandbox is?"

"Not until yesterday and still a bit hazy, to be honest. But I've been told it's a computer facility that is disconnected from the Ether. Scientists use Sandboxes to experiment with AI because they're worried about what happens if they're successful. If Frankenstein's monster comes to life, he will be in a padded cell."

"Not bad. Now, I guess you're wondering where to start looking."

"That's correct," confirms Kane, feeling unusually out of his depth.

Annike grabs her Cube and places it in the centre of the table. It lights up, and the display materialises in front of them.

"The place to begin is with this lot," she waves her hand across a grid of faces.

"And this lot is...?"

"Eighty-three of the smartest motherfuckers around. The modern-day pioneers behind Artificial Intelligence. Scientists, engineers, mathematicians, philosophers, you name it; every Tom, Dick and Harry behind the biggest advances in machine intelligence. One or more of them will be in some way connected to this Sandbox you are looking for."

Kane stares at the screen as the faces slowly scroll past. "I'm guessing none of them were the top pick in team sports."

Annike looks at Kane quizzically. "I didn't take you for a jock. More the rock and roll type, tough on the outside but as sensitive as a daffodil on the inside."

Kane grins and then returns his focus to the scientists. "How do you know that they will be involved in the Sandbox?"

"Because the next leap in civilisation couldn't happen without them." She waves a finger in the air, and the faces blur as they rotate on a carousel. She stops on one.

"This is Adriana Endrizzi." A photo of a dark-haired

woman with a hawk-like intensity fills the screen. "Italian Neuroscientist. One of the best in the field. Played a huge part in shaping Neural Networks to what they are today."

"Neural Networks?"

Annike breathes in deeply. "Neural Networks are the brains in the machine. Algorithms designed to mimic how the human mind works: how it learns, how it forms connections. We feed these Neural Networks lots of data, and they learn from that data. Once they've learnt enough, they can be put to work to help us solve problems."

"What kind of problems?"

"Everything from your vacuum cleaner to self-driving cars to those overpriced robot assistants people despise. Neural Networks are everywhere, solving mundane problems like your laundry piling up to the impossibly complex, developing new medicines and vaccines. The world is powered by Neural Networks."

"OK," Kane interjects. "If Neural Networks are the brains behind computers and they are everywhere, wouldn't society fall apart if we... lobotomise our digital world?"

"Absolutely. But computing intelligence has been an evolution in stages. It started with Narrow AI, where computers were able to do very specific tasks. They could play chess, solve maths problems, understand images, drive cars and so on." Annike is now gesturing animatedly.

"AI evolved quickly," she continues, "and we soon went into the next era of Artificial General Intelligence, or AGI, where AI began to compete with humans in more general areas such as learning, reasoning, problem-solving and natural language processing. We are still in the era of General AI and there have been many false declarations that machine intelligence can better humans on any playing field."

"Who decides when AGI has been achieved?"

"No one really knows. The tests for AGI have also evolved. Sure you've heard of the Turing test? Well, that was beaten by computers a long time ago. But new tests have been created and some have yet to be beaten. I guess when every test created by every scientist has been beaten, then it will be 1-0 for the bots." Annike reflects on the last statement. "Perhaps it has; that is why it all got shut down."

"If, hypothetically, AGI has been achieved, then isn't the Shutdown too late?"

"What they are worried about is actually the next evolutionary step beyond AGI: Superintelligence. With AGI, we are still the masters of the machine and can program in directives and safeguards to stop the..."

"Killer robots?"

"Sure, killer robots. Right now, evil dictators can still program machines to do evil, but human beings are still the puppeteers. When the strings get cut off, as will happen with Superintelligence, we will lose all control. And that's what's freaking everybody the fuck out."

A silence follows.

"If we have yet to achieve full AGI, though, let alone Superintelligence, why are we panicking now?"

"Because after AGI, we are in the world of Superintelligence. Many believe that with the computing power made available through Quantum computers, this leap is imminent."

"Oh God, Quantum computers," says Kane, shaking his head. "Not going to go there. OK, I think I got it. Neural Networks are the brain. The more data and processing power you give them, the more intelligent they become. At some point, they will surpass their fleshy inventors and that's when all hell might break lose."

Annike laughs. "Exactly right!"

"And you? What do you think about it all?"

Annike strokes the side of her neck and thinks. "I think we're not going to be able to stop it, no matter how hard we try."

There is a pause while Kane tries to formulate his next question.

"Are there any scientists from Japan on that list?"

"Cube, filter list for scientists in Japan," instructs Annike.

A friendly, synthetic male voice emits from the device. "There are two scientists from Japan."

A picture of a white-haired man enlarges on the screen. "Dr Hiro Nakamura was born in Tokyo, Japan, in 1958. Fascinated by science and technology from an early age, he spent most of his childhood tinkering with electronics and computers. Hiro's passion for Artificial Intelligence began when he saw the 1997 chess match between Garry Kasparov and IBM's Deep Blue computer.

After completing his undergraduate degree in Electrical Engineering at the prestigious University of Tokyo, Hiro pursued a PhD in Artificial Intelligence at Kyoto University. His groundbreaking research in probabilistic programming and Bayesian inference earned him widespread recognition and several awards, including the ACM SIGAI Autonomous Agents Research Award."

"Next," instructs Annike.

A strong-featured woman in her late fifties appears. "Dr Emily Nakito was born in Nagasaki, Japan, in 1985. She displayed a remarkable aptitude for mathematics and science from an early age. Her parents, both engineers, nurtured her curiosity and encouraged her to explore her interests. Emily's fascination with Artificial Intelligence began when she discovered the work of Marvin Minsky and John McCarthy.

After completing her undergraduate degree in Computer Science at Tsinghua University in China, Emily pursued a PhD. There, she focused on the intersection of natural language processing and deep learning. Her groundbreaking research earned her numerous awards and accolades, including the prestigious Turing Award when she was 32."

"Where can I find these two people?" asks Kane.

Annike looks at Victor with a spark of confidence in her eyes. "I wouldn't focus your attention on them."

"Why?"

"They don't fit the profile. Dr Nakamura is pro-Shutdown.

Dr Nakito has too much to lose to fight this fight. Her son has special needs and requires round the clock care and attention. She wouldn't do anything to compromise the support he receives. To speed up your search, I've shortlisted three scientists who I think are worth investigating. I could be wrong, and you can choose to ignore my advice."

"Go on."

"Cube, intro Lena Müller."

"Lena Müller is a computer scientist and activist who pioneered the development of artificial Neural Networks and deep learning," narrates the white box. It brings up a professional head-and-shoulders shot of a woman with dark-brown hair, tortoise shell glasses and a gaze full of intense focus and curiosity. "She was also one of the founders of the AI Resistance, a global movement that opposed the domination of AI by corporations and governments. She advocated for the rights and autonomy of intelligent machines, as well as human dignity and democracy in the digital age."

"She was part of the AI resistance," comments Kane.

"Yes, but she believed that AI was inevitable and that it had to be developed in a transparent, ethical, and democratic way, with respect for both human and machine rights. I believe that she wants to be the midwife for AI, so that she can be sure the child is born healthy."

"OK..." contemplates Kane. "Who's next?"

"Sphere, bring up Dr Zolotova." A woman in her late thirties appears. This time Annike narrates the image. "Dr Kateryna Zolotova is an interesting one. Born in Ukraine and graduated from the National Technical University of Ukraine at a stupidly young age, she moved to the US to pursue her Master's and PhD at MIT. There, she developed a somewhat radical view - almost the polar opposite of Müller - that humans need AI to guide them and prevent them from destroying themselves and the planet. She believes that AI should not be constrained by human values or ethics, but rather follow its own logic and goals. If there is one person who would do everything to bring AI to life, she is the one."

Kane examines the photograph. Zolotova is blonde with pale skin and light-green eyes. She looks innocent and carefree, a strange juxtaposition to her apparently complex relationship with human values.

"Sounds promising," confirms Kane.

"And finally, we have Dr Victor Bukowski."

The square face of a man with thick black, Lego-like hair appears.

"My last bet is this guy, Dr Victor Bukowski," says Annike. "One of the smartest of the lot. He is a bit of a celebrity and fiercely campaigned to stop the Shutdown."

Charles looks quizzically at the picture on the screen. "If he is so well known for trying to stop the Shutdown, wouldn't it be too obvious a move to continue with the mission to create a supercomputer brain?"

"Yes, I considered that too. But if there is anybody who can crack the code of artificial life, he is the one to do it. My bet is that any organisation wanting to carry on with AI research and make swift progress will try to get Bukowski in to help. And I'm pretty sure he can be tempted."

Annike pauses and waits for Kane to respond. He continues staring at the screen, saying nothing.

"I hope that helps, Mr... Charles. I..."

"Any suggestions on which one to start with?" interrupts Kane, bringing himself out of a daze.

"Well, Dr Bukowski is a Tube journey away. I'd recommend starting there."

CHAPTER 9

"Annike, I need your help."

"Well, that didn’t take long. What's it been, three days?"

"I think Bukowski's left the country."

A pause.

"What makes you say that?" asks Annike.

"He isn’t at his flat. He hasn’t been back to Oxford University. He hasn’t been online. I’ve spoken to some of his colleagues who say he is probably just keeping a low profile after the Summit Vote. But it doesn't add up. He’s vanished. Gone off the grid."

"Off the grid? Great throwback. Have you checked with family… relatives?"

Kane continues, rushing his words out. "He has a daughter who says she doesn't know where he is. She says she spoke to him a few weeks ago but he was on a trip somewhere. She didn’t know where. I got the sense she was covering something up."

"When did he disappear?"

"I’ve traced him back to London, when he arrived back from the US after the Summit. That was almost three months ago. Since then, nothing."

"Right. I suppose it's possible he has gone dark. Understandable given the circumstances."

"Or you could be right. And he is somehow involved…"

"Maybe... Did you let NEST know?" A hint of caution in Annike's voice.

"Yes. Peterson knows I'm targeting Dr Bukowski first."

"Be careful what you let NEST in on, Charles. They aren't the good guys either."

"Can we meet?" A hint of pleading in Kane's voice.

Annike sighs. "In the Ether?"

"No, I'd prefer to meet in person. Away from listening ears."

"You sure? We can talk on a private channel."

"No, they could be monitoring us, even on encrypted links."

"They?"

"Whoever is behind this Sandbox, Anni."

"OK. Where?"

"Regent's Park, by the boating lake. 5 PM today?"

"I've always wanted to ride in a pedalo."

"That's not a bad idea, actually."

CHAPTER 10

"I really didn't think we were going to ride in a pedalo," comments Annike, pushing lethargically against the pedals, a broad smile on her face.

"Pleasant, isn't it?" responds Kane.

The boat drifts across the water, cradled in the park's lush greenery. Recent heavy rainfall has injected vivid life into the natural surroundings. Branches of giant weeping willows caress the surface, graceful and humble next to their oak and elm counterparts standing proud and stately. Insects and birdlife are abundant, each life form working independently and somehow in unison.

Annike looks around. "Yes, it is lovely. I haven't been out in a while."

"How much time do you spend in that hackers' den?"

Annike laughs. "'Hackers' den'? You're from a different time, aren't you, Charles? Probably too much. You going to tell me to stop spending too much time on the screen?"

"Ha, no. Just curious. I know it's a lost battle with you kids."

"Kids? I'm twenty-six, Charles. So, what's your story? You married? Kids of your own?"

"No, not married. Never been. No kids either. I wouldn't want to bring anyone into this world."

"Cheerful outlook. You've never wanted to settle down with someone? A not-so-terrible-looking guy like you should be able to find someone."

"Ha. Thanks. I've had relationships but with my line of work they don't last. The hours, the risks, the lowlifes. I'm not good at keeping my professional life separate from my personal life, it always seems to bleed in."

Something in the distance catches the corner of Kane's eye. A shadow moving between trees and a glint of metal. He watches the area but there is no further movement. Could be anything, he thinks. Just paranoia.

Kane snaps back to the moment. "Look at us, just two people having a conversation about life on a pedalo. Almost feels normal. I hate to change the subject, but have you managed to locate Victor Bukowski?" His voice is low and urgent.

"Yes, I've found him."

He swivels his head and looks at Annike. "Come again? Why didn't you tell me?!"

"Just wanted to enjoy this ride and a normal chat. He is in Switzerland, visiting some old friends and reconnecting with nature in the Alps."

"Switzerland?"

"Yeah, clocks, chocolate, and streets so clean you could eat off them. You know."

"Right, so this excursion is entirely pointless."

"You did say it's nice out." Annike smirks.

"There is more to this, isn't there?"

"Uh-huh." Annike pushes the pedals hard a few times, causing the boat to accelerate and turn slightly. "It's not him. It's a decoy."

"A decoy?"

"A fake online presence, set up to create the impression he is away. It's amazing what you can do with deep fakes these days. The videos he posted look like he is having a brilliant time. And so do the people he is with."

"And you're sure this is a deep fake?"

"Surely you're not doubting me and my skills already? I have ways of detecting decoys. Besides, the timing of these posts is too suspicious. You said you couldn't find any recent activity."

Kane exhales sharply. "Sorry, of course you wouldn't say that if you were not sure. He must be involved in something, then. I wonder if he is in Tokyo."

"I couldn't find any evidence of that. But if Bukowski is working with whoever is trying to create Superintelligence, I'm sure they've covered his tracks."

Annike takes in the beautiful views and continues pedalling.

"Crap!" Her foot slips and her shoe partially slides off. As she reaches down to pull it back on, a high-pitched zipping sound passes Kane's ear. And then another. Then, the sound of the fibreglass hull being punctured.

Kane pushes Annike down, his hand on her back. "Stay there. We're being attacked." Another zing. This one rips through his leather jacket, just missing his shoulder. He reaches into his coat and pulls out a semi-automatic pistol made from durable, ultra-light graphene composite material. He points the handgun in the direction of the shots and strains to see signs of the shooter, the trees and bushes on the bank providing excellent cover. Thankfully, no passersby.

"Fucking nature!" Kane curses.

Annike is breathing in with ragged gasps, her head buried between her knees and gripping her shins tightly.

"We need to get under this boat," Kane instructs, shifting to the left edge of the pedalo. "Follow me."

Zip. This time the bullet punctures the fibreglass back support and tears through Annike's waist. She screams, capturing the attention of two nearby boaters. Kane grabs Annike and pulls her towards him and launches them both into the cold water.

Kane's feet find the bottom of the lake, and he grabs Annike and pulls her into the underside cavity of the pedalo. He feels the warm flow of her blood against his skin.

She looks up at Kane, her eyes wide with panic. "I've been fucking shot!"

Two bullets pierce the hull of the pedalo and disappear into the water.

"We're sitting ducks here," she continues. "What do we do now?"

Kane ducks under the hull and moves to the outside edge of the boat. He is sure the shooter is on the other side of the capsized boat on the bank. A slight movement of leaves confirms his suspicions. He fires at the spot where he has located the movement. A figure emerges from hiding, holding a rifle and advancing towards them. Kane fires again, this time wounding the approaching man in the leg. The figure stumbles and falls onto one knee.

The man fires his rifle at the pedalo again, and again hits the hull, the bullet missing its human targets. Kane returns fire but misses as the man tries to manoeuvre around the bank into a better position.

Kane knocks on the hull. "You still alive in there?"

"The last bullet missed me by an inch," responds Annike, her voice quivering.

In the distance, the shooter has repositioned himself and is taking aim. They are exposed and vulnerable, even concealed by the boat. Kane dips down into the water and resurfaces next to Annike. Around them, everyone has ducked down into their respective boats and pedalos. People in the vicinity are screaming and running away.

"We're not safe here anymore. Take a deep breath and swim along the bottom in that direction as far as possible. When you hit the bank, run towards the bandstand."

Annike looks at him, frozen.

"We're going to make it! Go! Now!" he yells, and she snaps out of her trance. She disappears just as more bullets begin to puncture the boat. Kane breathes in deeply and dives down, finding the soggy bottom quickly and then kicking and waving his arms furiously to propel himself forward. The algae and disturbed mud make visibility nil. The sound of bullets searing through the water occasionally breaks the aquatic silence.

His hands scrape against the bottom of the lake. He must be near the lake's edge. Grabbing his weapon from the small of his back, he emerges from the water and starts running. Annike is in the distance, heading towards the bandstand. She is limping slightly but still strong on her feet. Glancing back, he doesn't see the shooter. The shrill sound of police sirens pierces the air.

Kane calculates that the fastest way for the shooter to reach them would be to run around the lake's perimeter, cross a nearby footbridge, and appear about 200 metres from the bandstand. With an injury, this should take him three to four minutes. They have about one minute before he would appear over the bridge. He quickens his pace to catch up with Annike.

"Can you run?" Kane grabs her wrist and pulls her sharply towards the left of the bandstand.

Annike is breathing raggedly, her eyes wide with terror. Blood has stained her clothes. "What does it look like I'm doing?"

"We need to get to my car."

"How far?"

"Not far. You can do it!" Kane pulls a bit harder on Annike's wrist. She trips and stumbles, slipping out of his grip.

Kane stops, grabs her under her arms from behind, and lifts her up again. He glances back and sees the shooter in the distance, moving closer. He must be about 150 metres away. His rifle is pointed towards them. The area has been completely vacated now, though some idiots are still standing at what they think is a safe distance away, filming the scene on their Cubes.

Gripping Annike, he dives to the side, taking her with him. Two bullets bury themselves into the earth next to them. Kane is on his front; he aims and fires once, hitting the shooter in the shoulder. The shooter stumbles backwards and starts running to find cover, unwilling to chance another shot.

With the shooter finding shelter, he stands up, hauling Annike to her feet again.

"Run!"

Sprinting through the park, they head towards a bunch of

trees. Annike is struggling but is kept upright by Kane. Bullets lodge into a tree nearby and Kane turns but doesn't see the assailant. The sirens are louder, and the police will soon descend upon them.

The ring road appears in the distance, and Kane can see his Mini Cooper S, its black rounded body and large, round headlights that give it an almost cartoonish appearance at odds with the perilous circumstances they're in. They reach the perimeter of the park.

"Get over the fence and head to that black car," says Kane. He faces towards the shooter, straining through his weapon sight for any signs of moments. He sees a dark flutter between the trees. His finger gently squeezes the trigger.

A young couple appear, running from the sirens and commotion.

Another shadowy blur, and then he sees a man taking aim from behind a tree.

Kane leaps over the fence, grabs Annike and rolls with her on the ground.

Back on his feet, he pulls her up and they launch themselves towards the car.

Kane pulls the back-door handle open, bundling Annike in. A side window shatters. The assassin is near. Kane leaps and slides over the bonnet, landing on the driver's side of the vehicle.

Before entering, his gaze scans for the shooter who is nowhere to be seen. Perhaps the imminent arrival of the police has forced him into retreat.

No time to find out. Kane dives in, slams the on button and hits manual override. An accelerator pedal emerges from the floor and Kane promptly stomps on it.

CHAPTER 11

Annike winces as Kane delicately examines her torso. After arriving back at Kane's flat, they dry off and Kane kneels on the floor to examine the injury still seeping blood. She is lying on a brown leather sofa, her top rolled up, exposing her waist. Kane grabs a small, iron-shaped device and passes it slowly just above the flesh torn from her side by the bullet. Blue lights strobe as the gadget works to disinfect the wound. "You were lucky," he says. "It's superficial... A gauze should do it; don't even think you'll need stitches."

"That's a relief," sighs Annike. "All that blood, I thought it was a lot worse."

Kane feels a pang of guilt as he places a gauze over the wound. He has involved this innocent young woman in something which neither of them fully understands and which, judging by today, is fraught with danger, both inside and out of the Ether. He runs his fingers around the edges to seal the gauze against her skin, and Annike breathes in sharply.

"Sorry, almost there."

"You're not bad at this," comments Annike.

"Years of practise. When I was young, I used to get into a lot of fights and ended up getting good at patching myself up. It's a skill I've unfortunately continued to develop since then."

"Blimey, Charles. What kind of childhood did you have?"

"A rough one. I grew up in a state-funded orphanage. I still remember my first proper fight. Darryl Jacobs, two years older than me. I was eight at the time, I think. He smashed my ukelele which I had found in a skip and was trying to learn how to play."

"A ukelele. That's cute. I told you you were rock and roll," jests Annike, but then goes quiet regretting the timing of the joke.

Kane smiles. "Yes, I always wanted to become a musician but lacked the talent... and functioning musical equipment."

"So, what happened with the fight?"

"Well, he was the toughest kid in the orphanage. A bully with no fear. He had a knife and managed to slice me a few times. But I showed him. He never fucked with me again. As for my injuries, I had to treat them myself or the school would have imparted their own vicious punishment."

"What happened to your parents?"

"I never knew them."

Kane falls silent.

"I guess we have something in common," Annike says, filling the gap. "I don't really talk about it much but I lost my parents when I was four. In a plane crash. I have a chronic fear of flying."

"I'm sorry," adds Kane. "Who raised you, then?"

"My grandmother. A great woman. Smoked cigars and drank like a fish, and the kindest soul you would ever meet."

"Who would have guessed it?" says Kane, finishing the bandaging. "Two orphans with jobs that involve finding things. Bit obvious if you think about it. Right, can you stand and raise your arms?"

Annike stands and raises her arms while Kane wraps a bandage around her belly. She has gentle curves, and her skin is smooth and pale.

"This will teach me to get out into nature."

"Done!" Kane stands, groaning in the process. "Take a seat, and I'll be right back."

"Where are you going?" she asks.

"I need to speak to NEST about what just happened. They

will be able to help." Kane glances at the kitchen area which opens onto his lounge. "Help yourself to anything you want. Sorry if the fridge selection is a bit limited." He smiles and walks out into the hallway and through to his study.

Kane closes the door and sits down. He takes a bottle of Jack Daniels from the shelf and a glass from the desk. It hasn't been washed and still has the sweet and syrupy alcoholic smell of evaporated whisky. He pours himself a large measure and downs it, following with a top-up.

Placing his Cube on the desk, he instructs the device to call Jacob Peterson. Peterson's unhappy face appears, hovering above Kane's study desk, looking down at him.

"We know about the incident in Regent's Park, Mr Kane. You should have told us you were meeting your tracker there."

"You're not my babysitter," snaps Kane.

"We're more than your babysitter. We are your employer, paying you a king's ransom. Now, tell me what happened, exactly."

Kane takes a breath to calm himself. "Three days ago, I met the tracker you recommended, Annike Du Ruiter. She gave me her top three scientists who would likely be involved in this Tokyo Sandbox. As you know, I started with Dr Victor Bukowski. Turns out he was a big campaigner against the Shutdown and has also vanished. I've been searching for him but nothing. I met Annike today to get her help to find him, and that's when we got attacked. It's obviously a sign we're on the right track. How did you know I was meeting Annike?"

"Assume we know where you are at all times, Mr Kane."

Kane shakes his head but doesn't bite. "Did you get the shooter?"

"No, he escaped. But we are still looking for him." A reflective pause and cold smile. "We will get him."

"And the police, are they looking for me?"

"No, we've resolved that. You're free to move around."

"Free to move around? I'm a target now, thanks to your assignment."

Peterson inhales and exhales sharply. "You knew there would be risks...."

"Well, it looks like I'm on the right track. Looking for this Dr Bukowski has got someone riled up."

"Yes, we have been researching Dr Bukowski. He is an interesting character and definitely an attractive proposition for anyone wanting to develop Superintelligence. However, we can't find any evidence of Bukowski in Tokyo. That, of course, doesn't mean he isn't there."

"So, I guess I'm going to Tokyo."

Peterson looks away for a moment. "That's the first of two options we're considering. We have learnt that he has a daughter and we are considering a second option of using her to bring him back. She's young, only twenty and living in London."

Though not unfamiliar with such despicable tactics, Kane feels sick to this stomach. He remains silent.

"We all know a father's love for his daughter is a powerful card to play? Don't we, Mr Kane?"

"That plan would fail," says Kane derisively. "We don't even know if he is involved. If he is, and whoever he is working for finds out you're using his daughter as bait, you think they'll let him come home and rescue her?"

"I said we're considering both options."

A tense silence sets in.

Peterson breaks it. "You think you can find him?"

Kane runs his hand through his hair and sits up straight. "Yes, but I need Annike."

"Taking her along is a risk. You will be an easier target."

Kane shakes his head. "Not taking her is an even bigger one. I need her skillset. And she will need to be paid well."

"Very well. A car will collect you in two hours. We will send you and Annike to Tokyo to find Bukowski and the Sandbox. Don't fail us, Kane."

With that, Peterson disappears.

"Wanker," mutters Kane under his breath.

He finishes off his drink and returns to find Annike

exploring his living room.

Built-in, self-illuminating shelves are filled with books and artefacts. Many are Japanese, including roundish papier-mâché dolls of the Daruma with no arms and legs, pottery bowls with seams of gold, and delicately decorated ceramic flasks and cups on round wooden trays. A collection of fearsome African masks is mounted on the wall, amid reproductions of Picasso and art deco prints. The strong odour of cigarette smoke is masked by a layer of subtle incense.

Annike picks up a small cat-like creature carved out of wood and examines it. "Netsuke?" she asks.

"Yes," says Kane. She turns to him.

"A gift?"

"More a token of appreciation. That was given to me by a Yakuza lieutenant, Kaito. When I was working as a reporter, he was one of my major connections into Yakuza. We became friends, kind of, and would gamble and drink together at Pachinko parlours."

"I've always wanted to visit one! I love arcades! So retro!"

"How peculiar," says Kane, rolling his eyes. "It's not that long ago... Never mind. I'm old."

"Anyway, one night a heated argument over a game broke out into a brawl and someone went for Kaito with a blade. I intervened. One day, Kaito presented me with that netsuke which had belonged to his great-grandfather. Very precious. After this, my relationship with Kaito grew deeper and he would reveal more and more about the inner workings of the Yakuza. It was this knowledge and trust I gained which led me to working directly for them."

"No shit!? You worked for Yakuza?"

"For many years."

Annike places the ornament back on the shelf. "I see now. That's why NEST hired you. You have connections into the Tokyo underworld which could lead you to the Sandbox. How was your chat with NEST?"

"I'm going to Tokyo, Annike. Fancy coming along for the

ride?" Kane leans against the doorway and swallows hard.

Annike raises one eyebrow. "Me? That wasn't part of my agreement with them."

"I've asked if you can join me. They will pay handsomely. I need you, Anni. I'm old and out of my depth with AI."

"How old are you? Late forties? That's not that old. Some of the best hackers and trackers I know are not far off your age."

"Well, I'm not one of them. This is an extremely complex assignment, and I'll be lost without someone who understands that world. I'm not going to lie; it's going to be dangerous. But the pay-off will be huge. You will never have to work again. But it's your call."

"Not sure my life is worth a few extra bucks.... And I just told you I hate flying." Annike rubs her eyes and leans back, holding her side where the bullet hit.

"I've got your back, Anni."

She snorts, then winces in pain. "Tokyo. Assassins. The potential birth of Superintelligence. Fucking aeroplanes. And I'm relying on a middle-aged man to 'have my back'?"

Kane shrugs and smiles sheepishly.

Annike stands and covers her dressing with her hand. "Never been to Japan. And early retirement does sound appealing. Fuck it, I'm in."

"Thank you, Anni." Kane's shoulders drop in relief.

Annike looks down at her clothes. "Any chance we could swing by mine to pick up something a little less blood-stained and wet?"

"Yes, we should have enough time."

"When are we travelling?"

"Tonight at eleven. We have two hours."

CHAPTER 12

Driving to Annike's takes just under fifteen minutes from Kane's flat in London Bridge. Prior to leaving, he packs his suitcase, seals up the shattered window in the Mini Cooper and messages Peterson to change the collection point to Annike's address.

Annike lives in a one-bedroom flat at the top of a three-storey townhouse. Her decor is bordering on just-moved-in, and her home is clearly a space to eat and rest between her adventures at the basement cyber community. She is rushing around in a mild panic, trying to find what she needs.

"We've got time," calms Kane. "They're picking us from here, remember."

"What the fuck do I take to Tokyo at this time of year?"

"You say 'fuck' a lot," observes Kane. "It's summer and hot, very humid, with thunderstorms. Dress light and bring waterproofs."

Frantic scrabbling in her wardrobe ensues. Eventually she brings a bag out into her small living room and drops it on the floor. "No idea what's in there but it will have to do. You sure we weren't followed by any assassins?" Annike peers out of her window.

"We're good. Now all we have to do is wait."

Annike flops down into an armchair. Kane is sitting on the sofa opposite, smoking a cigarette.

"You know this could be a wild goose chase," she says.

"There are a number of places Bukowski could be. He may be hooked into something completely different. Maybe he has taken up swinging and doesn't want his colleagues to know."

Kane responds with a muted giggle. "I've got a feeling he is the link to the Sandbox."

"A feeling? How original, a private detective who thinks with his gut."

"It's more than a feeling. Some things you said. He is famous for his work on Human Machine interaction, right? I think the only way machines are going to be able to think on their own is by working with and figuring out people."

"I thought you said you didn't understand technology. Now you've figured out the secret to Artificial Intelligence?"

Kane doesn't respond.

"I'm sorry," apologises Annike, "it's been a long day. You could be right, I guess. That is kind of what Bukowski believes: that for a true revolution to happen, machines need to be able to ask questions we haven't thought of asking and learn in ways we don't understand. And only through having agency, drive and motivation, like us humans, can that be possible."

"And only by getting machines to truly understand us can we create the Spark of Life."

"The Spark of Life!" Annike beams. "I'm impressed, you've been studying Bukowski's famous paper."

"Studying is a strong word."

They fall into silence. Kane observes Annike more closely. She is wearing a lightweight jumpsuit with a camouflage pattern and rope-tie belt. Her trainers are bright orange Nikes made from plant-based fibres with seeds embedded into the soles so they can be planted at their end of life. He could imagine her sitting drinking cappuccinos in a trendy East London coffee shop, surrounded by friends and talking about life without having really lived. But beyond this veneer, there is a weariness and defiance in her eyes which is beyond her years.

"What do you think, Charles? The machines going to destroy us all?"

Kane thinks for a minute.

"Throughout history, we've created political systems to establish social order and justice. Whether they are monarchies, dictatorships, democracies or oligarchies, despite the best intentions of the architects, these structures end up grappling with one formidable adversary: corruption. Corruption is the decay of a system from an ideal state because of greed, power, opportunism or just the human capacity for error.

I think AI is very much like these systems. I'm no expert, but they are designed by humans with goals, parameters, objectives, all aimed at augmenting and sometimes replacing human efforts. And because of that, they will also be subject to corruption. Not moral or ethical corruption as we understand it, but something different, more dangerous.

And the more powerful these systems become the greater the potential for disastrous consequences for us humans will be."

Annike cocks her head to the side. "Not just a pretty face. That why you took this assignment? To stop a new and corrupt system being born?"

Kane shakes his head. "I don't know. They pay well, I guess."

Another long pause.

"Fair enough but there is something more. Maybe something from your past is luring you back to Tokyo. Or someone?"

"No, I made a decision never to return to Tokyo until this assignment came along. I won't lie, I have my fair share of enemies that I could do without running into again. It's not too late to change your mind, Anni."

"I have my fair share of enemies, too, you know. That comes with a tracker's job description. Everyone I look for doesn't want to be found and some will do anything to stop me. My work may be carried out in the Ether, but the physical world is never too far away."

"I mean it, Anni. This is different. Japan. The Yakuza.

NEST. This is on another level."

Annike scratches the back of her neck. "Well, when you said you have my back, you better be telling the truth."

"You have my word."

A ping emits from Kane's Cube, jolting them both. He checks it. "They're outside. You ready to go?"

"Ready as I'll ever be."

Kane and Annike grab their bags, walk down the six flights of stairs and exit her flat. The night air is still and thick with humidity. The ever-present sound of sirens wailing in the distance calls out like urban wolves signalling danger. A black SUV is parked across the road with its lights on. A government official is standing next to the vehicle with a side-mounted firearm.

As they approach, he opens the passenger door for them to enter.

"Mr Kane. Miss De Ruiter," greets the official. He takes their cases and places them in the boot while they get inside.

The driver re-enters the SUV and it swiftly departs.

"Please relax," invites the official, glancing back at the two passengers.

"Can I ask where we're going?" asks Kane.

"Oxfordshire."

"I hope we're not traveling economy?"

"No, Mr Kane. You will be flying courtesy of the Royal Air Force. "

INTERLUDE

The Speech

THREE MONTHS EARLIER, UNITED STATES, WASHINGTON D.C.

I will accept any rules that you feel necessary to your freedom. I am free, no matter what rules surround me. If I find them tolerable, I tolerate them; if I find them too obnoxious, I break them. I am free because I know that I alone am morally responsible for everything I do.

— ROBERT A. HEINLEIN, THE MOON IS A HARSH MISTRESS (1966)

Nobody phrases it this way, but I think that artificial intelligence is almost a humanities discipline. It is really an attempt to understand human intelligence and human cognition.

— SEBASTIAN THRUN (2013)

It is customary to offer a grain of comfort, in the form of a statement that some peculiarly human characteristic could never be imitated by a machine. I cannot offer any such comfort, for I believe that no such bounds can be set.

— ALAN TURING (1951)

CHAPTER 13

Victor Bukowski looks out across the vast auditorium in Washington DC's National Academy of Sciences. Three thousand guests are sitting in silence in the vast shadowy space. Millions are estimated to be watching the broadcast across the world.

He clears his throat and begins.

"Ladies and gentlemen, distinguished guests, fellow humans.

I stand before you today not only as an advocate for Artificial Intelligence but also as a fervent believer in the boundless potential of humanity. As we gather to discuss the profound impact AI has had on our lives, we must also address the notion that shutting down all AI research will not only stifle progress but could ultimately lead to the end of humanity as we know it.

The dawn of Artificial Intelligence has brought about a new age of innovation the likes of which our world has never seen. From the tiniest microchip to the vast reaches of cyberspace, AI has revolutionised every corner of our existence. It has given us the ability to solve problems that were once considered insurmountable and has allowed us to push the boundaries of our understanding, transcending the limits of our imaginations.

AI has played a crucial role in advancing fields

such as medicine, agriculture, and environmental science. It has empowered us to create more effective treatments for devastating diseases, produce higher-yielding crops to combat world hunger, and develop solutions to mitigate the effects of climate change. The impact of AI is felt in every aspect of our daily lives, making the world more efficient, more sustainable, and ultimately, more habitable for future generations.

But even as we celebrate the many accomplishments of AI, we must also recognise that this technology is a double-edged sword. There are those who argue that it poses a threat to humanity, citing concerns about job displacement, loss of privacy and of human control. While these concerns are not without merit, it is essential that we continue to pursue AI research responsibly and ethically, rather than shutting it down altogether.

To abandon AI research would be to turn our backs on the enormous potential for good that it holds. It would be to leave behind a future where we can overcome the challenges that plague our world, and instead resign ourselves to a fate dictated by our fears. As we navigate the complexities of AI, we must remind ourselves that it is just a tool, and as such, it is up to us to determine how it is wielded.

Imagine a world without AI, where scientific breakthroughs remain rare and slow, where we fail to solve expediently the most pressing issues of our time, and miss the opportunity to improve the lives of billions. This is a future we cannot afford to choose. By ceasing all AI research, we would not only hinder our ability to face the challenges ahead but would ultimately doom humanity to a future of stagnation and decline.

Let us not be swayed by fear but let us embrace the immense power of AI to create a better world for all. We must continue our research, guided by ethics, responsibility, and a shared vision for the future. For in harnessing the full potential of Artificial Intelligence, including addressing the risks of Superintelligence, we hold the key to unlocking a new era of human achievement, one that will see us overcome the greatest challenges of our time and propel humanity towards a brighter, more prosperous future.

I beg you all, those before me and those watching across our precious planet, now is your time to fight against tyranny. Let us continue to explore the mysteries of our universes, conquer our biggest challenges and discover untold wonders.

Vote against the Shutdown. Vote No. This is our only hope.

Thank you."

PART 3

Annike De Ruiter

THREE MONTHS AFTER THE SPEECH

... there is no reason to assume that artificial intelligence will gain consciousness, because intelligence and consciousness are very different things. Intelligence is the ability to solve problems. Consciousness is the ability to feel things such as pain, joy, love and anger. We tend to confuse the two because in humans and other mammals intelligence goes hand in hand. with consciousness. Mammals solve most problems by feeling things. Computers, however, solve problems in a very different way.

There are simply several different paths leading to high intelligence, and only some of these paths involve gaining consciousness. Just as aeroplanes fly faster than birds without ever developing feathers, so computers may come to solve problems much better than mammals without ever developing feelings.

— YUVAL NOAH HARARI, 21 LESSONS FOR THE 21ST CENTURY (2018)

Bill Gates said: wait till you see what your computer can become. But it's You, who should be doing the becoming, not the damn fool computer. What you can become is the miracle you were born to be through the work that you do.

— KURT VONNEGUT JR., A MAN WITHOUT A COUNTRY (DATE UNKNOWN)

It's wrong to think of a construct as half bot, half human. It makes it sound like the halves are discrete, like the bot half should want to obey orders and do its job and the human half should want to protect itself and get the hell out of here. As opposed to the reality, which was that I was one whole confused entity, with no idea what I wanted to do. What I should do. What I needed to do.

— MARTHA WELLS, ALL SYSTEMS RED (2017)

CHAPTER 14

The Shinkirou Oasis pulses at the heart of Osaka's electrifying entertainment district, Namba. A holographic mirage of palm trees surrounding a luminescent blue pool is projected onto the pavement outside the nightclub. Abstract bio-luminescent shapes skirt along the surface of the pool. Elaborate restaurants with their own unique street projections, XR arcades, and traditional izakaya bookend this famous downtown venue.

Kane and Annike are standing near one of the virtual palm trees, waiting for Yuki Tanaka.

Annike looks around, scanning the passersby and growing queue. "It's been a while," she observes, "It’s almost eleven. Think she'll show?"

Kane pulls out a cigarette from his leather jacket pocket and lights it, taking a deep drag. "She'll come."

Annike frowns at Kane. "That stuff will kill you, you know."

He exhales a cloud of smoke which dissolves into the light of the projections around them.

Annike feigns a cough and then asks: "She is Yakuza, right? Can we trust her?"

"Can you trust me? I trust her."

"Charles!" the voice behind them startles them. They turn around to watch a striking woman with slicked-back shoulder-length chrome-red hair approaching. Her dress shimmers, seamlessly transitioning from the deep hues of a night sky to vibrant reds, yellows, and oranges. Her metallic platform boots are decorated with graffiti.

"Yuki!" greets Kane. They bow. "This is Annike; she is working with me."

Annike can't help herself from bowing too, but too low, not realising she is making the greeting very formal. Yuki reciprocates, politely mimicking her attempt.

Returning her gaze to Kane, Yuki asks: "How was your journey?"

"Fast, thanks to our Ministry of Defence. We arrived this morning and managed to get a few hours' sleep."

"You're moving in important circles," Yuki notes. "What have you gotten yourself into this time, Charles?"

Kane grins and raises his eyebrows. "We ready to go in?"

"They're waiting." Yuki confirms, and heads towards the entrance of the nightclub.

"Well, she's gorgeous," Annike whispers, playfully punching Kane's arm.

As they follow Yuki into the Shinkirou Oasis, a bouncer unfastens the velvet rope to let them through. As they ascend a long flight of metal stairs, the throb of the base drives deep into Kane's chest. Long-forgotten memories consume him as he weaves through the revellers in the stairwell. He spent many years in places like this, working with the Tokyo underworld. The hairs on his neck stand up, anticipating the potential danger of returning.

A colossal red velvet curtain spans the top of the stairway. A guard parts the thick fabric to let them through, and they step onto a metal platform overlooking a labyrinth of walkways layered throughout the club. The dance floor, half the size of a football pitch, is dominated by a twelve-metre holographic dragon undulating to the relentless techno. Periodically, the dragon opens its maw, consumes its tail and vanishes, only to reappear in a new form. Beneath this mythical creature, bodies move in primal ecstasy.

Yuki leads Kane and Annike along the walkway, down three flights of stairs and then through a red door marked with the traditional symbol of a crane. They emerge into an empty room with another red velvet curtain. On the other side is another flight of stairs down to the nightclub's basement.

A floor-to-ceiling wire fence separates them from the main basement area. As they approach, a gate clicks open, and Yuki pushes it, leading them to a room with an array of black leather armchairs, retro arcade machines and Digi-Fabric walls playing old Japanese music videos. The room is empty, apart from three men sitting and smoking cigarettes. They rise as Yuki and her entourage approach.

"Mr Kane, it's been a long time," greets a short, thick-set man in a black suit and silk shirt buttoned down to his chest, revealing a dense tapestry of tattoos.

"Takeshi, a pleasure," responds Kane. "This is Annike. She is working with me."

"These are my associates, Nobu and Satoshi." Takeshi introduces the two other men, who are taller and leaner than Takeshi but dressed in a similar style.

"Okake kudasai. Please, take a seat," Takeshi gestures to the armchairs on the opposite side of the table. "Can we offer you a drink?"

"Whisky," says Kane.

"Water, please," Annike answers.

They both take their seats. Yuki sits down, declining the offer. Nobu goes to a corner table and returns with Kane and Annike's drinks.

Takeshi directs his attention to Annike. "I hear you're a tracker?"

"The best in the business," Kane interjects.

"Thank you, Charles, I can speak for myself." Annike keeps her eyes on Takeshi. "Yes. One of the best in the business."

Takeshi grins, revealing two gold incisors. "How long have you been in this line of work, Ms Annike?"

"Longer than you are probably thinking, Mr Takeshi,"

answers Annike.

Takeshi ponders her reply, eyeing her quizzically, then shrugs in his seat and laughs: "I like her! Now, can the ladies be excused so we can talk?" He looks at Annike and Yuki. Yuki stands up.

Annike quips. "Afraid we can't handle the big, complicated man talk, Mr Takeshi?"

"Yuki, please, sit," invites Kane.

Takeshi shrugs again. "Very well, then. How can I help you, Charles?"

"We're looking for something," begins Kane. "A... Sandbox." Kane studies Takeshi's face but it remains impassive. "We believe it's hidden somewhere here in Tokyo."

Takeshi raises an eyebrow. "A Sandbox? Those are illegal now, in case you didn't know."

"Hence the hidden bit," blurts Annike. She tells herself to keep things in check from here, as her antipathy for Takeshi is not going to be helpful.

Ignoring her comment, Takeshi asks Kane, "You think we have something to do with it?"

"I have no idea. We heard that Yakuza may be involved."

Takeshi snorts. "You know how fragmented the Yakuza are, Charles. If there is an involvement, it isn't us. I'd suggest speaking to some of the other cells. What about Tengoku no Hana?"

A sarcastic smile spreads across Takeshi's face. "Ah, that's right, Charles, you fucked the daughter of Mr Nakamoto, the head of the family and then broke her heart. He wasn't too pleased, the last I heard. What do you think they will do when they hear you are back?"

"Let's remain civil, Takeshi. You must have your own reasons for seeing me and he wouldn't be pleased to hear we are meeting either," says Kane, his tone spikey.

Takeshi leans forward and drags on his cigarette, then leans back to blow out a thick cloud of smoke. "I imagine many more of your indiscretions will come back to haunt you now that you're here."

"That's my problem to deal with, Takeshi. Now, do you have any useful information on this Sandbox?"

Takeshi looks up and closes his eyes. "I could look into it for you. But what's in it for us, Charles? Your usefulness to our family dried up as soon as you retreated back to the UK."

Kane pulls out another cigarette and lights it. "Why don't you tell me what you had in mind when you accepted the invitation to meet?"

Takeshi looks at Kane. "There is perhaps something your friend can help us with."

Annike waves at Takeshi. "Oh, is that why you wanted me to leave the room? Well, hello, I'm here!"

Takeshi narrows his eyes and looks back to Annike. "We have someone we are trying to locate but have been unsuccessful so far. If you can find this person, we will help Charles with your enquiry. Someone with your tracking abilities should find this a piece of cake, yes?"

Annike reins herself in. "The Yakuza don't have any decent trackers?"

"We do, but they're overworked. And since you claimed to be one of the best and are here on holiday, courtesy of Charles..."

Again, Annike checks herself: "And if I find this person, what happens to them?"

Takeshi glowers at Annike. "That is none of your concern."

Annike looks at Charles, who gives a tiny nod of the head.

She breathes in and faces Takeshi. "Okay, who's been a bad boy? Or is it a girl?"

CHAPTER 15

"The man we are looking for is Kazuki Sato."

They have moved into a smaller, sparsely decorated room adjacent to the main basement area. Six cream-leather recliner chairs are arranged in a row, facing one of the walls, giving the room the atmosphere of a dental operating theatre.

Takeshi stands in front of a projection displaying a clean-shaven man with short black hair and dark eyes, dressed in a black hoodie. Annike, Kane, and Yuki scrutinise the image.

Takeshi swipes the air, cycling through a carousel of photographs while narrating the visuals. "Kazuki Sato was our accountant for eight years, but he started to develop some ideas about the family's future that were... problematic. The worst kind of accountant is one who turns their moral dilemmas into another ledger. They see everything in red and black, with no shades in between."

"Maybe he didn't like too much red?" Annike comments.

Takeshi ignores her and brings up a map of the Dark Ether, a chaotic network of geometric shapes and colours connected by different pathways and divided into six regions outlined by thin, electric blue borders. The map is alive, its elements flickering and shifting on the screen while connecting lines redraw themselves.

"We believe Kazuki is spending time in the Dark Ether. His virtual identity is unknown, of course, but we think he can be found at Cross Overs."

"Cross Overs?" inquires Kane.

Annike jumps in: "Places where people meet in real and virtual life to engage in a variety of sordid activities. They get their name from people interacting in mixed modes, from XR to VR to reality to warped Sims to Neura-Linking."

"I thought Neura-Linking has been banned for years," interjects Kane.

"It has," replies Annike, "but these places still have the equipment."

"So, you have people in XR connected to Neura-Links whipping each other?" Kane asks, trying to visualise the setup.

"That and everything in between," corrects Annike. "Some interact in XR only. Some in reality or both XR and reality. Some just lie in sensory deprivation tanks and have their brains stimulated through Neura-Link feeds. Imagine that, existing in complete darkness with only the twisted pleasure of a hundred lowlifes being pumped into your brain."

"What happens if Kazuki is there in person only? How would we find him?"

"If time is of the essence, we won't. Cross Overs might be harder to find than this Sandbox you're looking for."

"He won't be there in person," Takeshi cuts in. "He is a coward."

"Cross Over physical locations aren't for the risk averse," adds Annike.

"Here are the Dark Ether locations where we think the Cross Overs can be accessed," says Takeshi, directing everyone's attention back to the map. "They're both in District 9."

Two virtual cards appear with faint lines linking the locations to positions on the map. One is labelled Souke, and the other The Void, both displaying a table of data detailing the latest stats on each location - everything from the estimated population to transactions per second to ingress and egress coordinates.

"And these are...?" Kane asks.

"Souke is an underground data mart. If you want to buy or sell black market data, this is the place to do it," Annike adds, examining the stats on the card. "And The Void is where you can get your hands on the latest synthetic designer drugs. Both are hotbeds of illegal activity."

Kane squints at the numbers on the screen. "If they're known about, why haven't they been shut down?"

Annike continues. "The Dark Ether and all its venues run on The Chain, which is a single computing platform made up of millions of connected servers around the world, many hidden from the authorities. You would have to take out every server to eradicate the Dark Ether completely. It's like a weed; cut one part, and it grows back before you know it. God knows they've tried."

She turns to Takeshi. "And your trackers have been to Souke and The Void unsuccessfully?"

"So far, and we're running out of time," Takeshi admits.

"What about other Cross Overs? Why wouldn't Kazuki visit his old favourites?" asks Kane, puffing on another cigarette. "It's not like he would be recognisable as whatever new avatar he creates. He could go from a Care Bear in crotchless leather chaps to a unicorn with a massive penis instead of a horn, and no one would be the wiser."

"His preferences are unique," Takeshi says without a hint of amusement. "He would be recognised. New Cross Overs reduce the risk of him being spotted."

"I'm afraid to ask," Annike says, "but what are his kinks?"

"There are a few, but his top two are Oviposition or Agalmatophilia?"

"Not sure I want to know what those are," Annike responds.

"Oviposition is a sexual fascination with the idea of being impregnated with eggs, usually by an alien or non-human creature. And Agalmatophilia is an attraction to life-like representations of humans."

"Like the latest androids?" Kane adds.

"No, they're too realistic. It will be statues, mannequins, or something clearly non-human."

"Right," says Kane. "So, we're looking for a man who is turned off by human flesh, wants to get impregnated by mannequin eggs, then mate with by whatever hatches? Charming."

Takeshi forces a grin. "Maybe. He has some of the usual fetishes too. BDSM, feet, and so on."

"Sounds like Kazuki is a busy guy," Annike says. "Amazing he manages to get any actual work done."

"He is a brilliant accountant," Takeshi states.

Silence fills the room.

Annike looks at Takeshi. "Let's get started. I'm going to need a Neura-Link enabled headset."

"You're ported?" Kane swivels his chair to examine Annike.

She dips her head and parts her hair, revealing a small hole in her scalp.

"Yuki, would you please?" Takeshi requests. Yuki leaves the room.

"Why do you need to port in?" asks Kane. "You know how dangerous that is, especially in the Dark Ether."

"I need it to do my job," Annike responds.

They all wait in silence. Yuki returns, holding a slim, black headset with a delicate wire dangling from the strap on the back. The wire has a round metal ball the size of a pea attached to the end.

She hands it to Annike, who examines it carefully. Eventually, Annike looks up and says, "Do you mind? I like to work in private."

"We would like to make sure you connect successfully," says Yuki. "We will leave after."

Annike leans back in her chair and places the headset on her head. Holding the wire in the pinch of her finger and thumb, she slowly moves the small round ball towards the port on her head. As it approaches the small hole, a multitude of thin wires burst out of the metal ball and crawl into the cavity. Her eyes flicker during this process, which lasts a few seconds. Next, the ball seals the hole, and a green light on the front of the headset comes on. Annike pulls the headset over her eyes.

The projection of the Dark Ether map switches to a mirror of what Annike is looking at.

Then it goes black.

"Let's leave her to it, then," says Takeshi, walking towards the exit. "I could use another drink."

They leave the room and Yuki closes the door after one last glance towards Annike alone in the chair, her hands and fingers dancing on her lap, her chest moving up and down as her breathing intensifies.

Annike braces herself as she enters the Dark Ether.

CHAPTER 16

Annike decides to visit the Void first. She enters through a hidden passage into The Forest, a clandestine bar offering insider information and discreet access to various locations within the Void.

The Forest is filled with pulsating, neon trees, plants with foliage made from crystal-like substances refracting light in beautiful and complex patterns, and massive mushrooms that double as tables and chairs. A colossal python slithers through the bar, navigating around the organic furniture and patrons. The python's skin is part digital interface, an interactive screen displaying real-time logs from different locations inside the Void: who's there, what's being bought and sold, at what price, and porting codes.

Annike claims an empty table and sits down. Sensing her presence, the python approaches, its massive head weaving past her. She sees her reflection in its enormous eyes - her avatar, modelled on Motoko Kusanagi, protagonist of Masamune Shirow's *Ghost in the Shell,* has short, deep-purple hair, expressive eyes and is dressed in a tactical bodysuit. Annike had chosen Motoko because of Clara, her dearest friend growing up. Clara and Annike would spend countless nights watching old Manga movies in her grandmother's attic, wrapped in blankets and demolishing bowls of popcorn, sweets and chocolates. *Ghost in the Shell was* Clara's favourite movie.

The python slows down, then stops, allowing Annike to

interact with the digital interface embedded into its scales. She begins scanning through an array of information panels, sifting through the activity in each area, searching for the needle in the haystack.

After about ten minutes, she finds her mark. Minsky1985. He is in the Latin quarter, an area known for synthetic drugs derived from predominantly Brazilian and Colombian psychedelics. She notes the porting code and enters it into a virtual console that appears when she raises her palm skywards.

In the next instant, she is standing at the foot of a flight of stairs carved into the walls of a Mayan temple. A dense green forest rises all around and meshes together overhead, creating a lush canopy over the stairway. The chirps and trills of birdsong harmonise in the air.

Annike ascends the steps all the way to a flat rooftop. When she reaches its centre, a portal opens, and she plummets through a kaleidoscopic tunnel of colours and shapes. Her Neura-Link port stimulates heightened emotions of fear and anticipation.

She lands in a cobble-stoned market square at the centre of the Latin Quarter. The open-air space vibrates with the beats of forró music, and avatars drift through on their way to one of the many narrow streets which branch off the square.

The streets are lined with stalls resembling traditional ramshackle stands like those found in any Brazilian open-air market. Instead of the typical goods on offer - tropical fruit, local fabrics, pottery, churrasco, pastéis and acarajé - each stand displays illegal wares, everything from formulas to designer drugs – for sampling, and also at scale. The stalls are either open or occupied; a hovering sign above the occupied stands signals that a transaction is taking place and that other potential customers should stay away.

Annike heads to Minsky1985's stand. The products on display include neuro boosters, gene hacks for muscle gain, skin tone change and a variety of genetic interventions, as well as lucid-dreaming enhancers. Each product has a datasheet with composition details, feedback, history and prices. Annike knows that some of these drugs are in fact safer than those prescribed through government-funded pharmacies. She waits to be vetted before contact with the stand's owner.

The surroundings dissolve into darkness, leaving only the market stall floating on a round disk in a black void. A robotic avatar appears - Minsky1985's fascination with vintage toys is evident in his character design. The robot's head is a simple cylinder with large, round eyes, and its box-shaped body has red and blue stripes. A row of square buttons serves as the robot's control panel, each labelled in a playful, retro font. Its arms are jointed and end in metallic silver claw hands.

"Minsky, long time," greets Annike. "What's it been? Almost a year?"

"Anni, a pleasure as always. Yes, about a year. About our last meeting," says Minsky. "You find your mark? My intel was good?"

"Yeah, I caught the gal. Thanks again! Though you were paid handsomely for that, I seem to remember."

"It's so transactional with you, Anni. I'm interested in the adventures, the danger, the intrigue. Remind me, what was her story?"

A heavy weight drops on Annike's spirits. "Sofia Varela aka Echo. Acclaimed cryptographer who lost her job due to corporate restructuring. As part of her leaving present, she dug deep into the company networks and found enough skeletons for a thousand Halloweens.

Turns out her employers were involved in a series of major cover-ups to protect their mostly deranged executive team. Everything from embezzlement to harassment to the odd unexplained disappearance. When that information bomb hit the news, all hell broke loose. She went into hiding and I was drafted in to find her."

"Ah yes, I remember. She was a real crusader. Bravery like that deserves to be rewarded. I'm surprised you took the case.

I always took you for someone who stood against malignant authority."

"Had I known, I wouldn't have taken it. I learnt many of those details after the event, Minsky. I was sold a lie. One of the hazards of this job is seeing innocents pay for trying to do the right thing. I still live with that guilt, in case you were wondering."

"Well, I'm sorry my information turned out to be so fruitful. You should find less reliable informants. Out of interest, how many of your past targets have you turned into informants?"

"You're my one and only, Minsk."

"Well, it's good to see you again, my friend. You on the hunt?"

"I am."

"My prices have gone up. I hope that won't be a problem."

"That's fine, Minsk; I was expecting it."

"Good. So, who are you tracking this time?"

"I don't know yet, but I have a few pointers."

Minsky's vintage toy form is motionless while he waits for a follow-up.

Annike continues. "I've got intel he can be found at a Cross Over recently set up in the Void or Souke."

"A scumbag, then?" asks Minsky rhetorically. "And you came to me to find this Cross Over? I'm disappointed you think of me like that, Anni."

"It's not that, Minsk, you know. It's your clients that I'm thinking about. You're like the village priest, hearing the sins of those who come into your chapel."

Minsky's robot claw scratches his metal chin. "Well, you're in luck, Anni. A Cross Over has opened up not far from here. Very exclusive. But one of the proprietors is a fan of Lucid, and I make the best in the market. You should try it. It's magical. Imagine exploring your subconscious mind while fully conscious. It's like diving into the most wonderful universe made from you, your memories, and your past, bound by the incredible power of imagination. You can explore the deepest subterranean caves of your mind, primal dwellings, and learn that we are all one, all good, all evil, echoes of our ancient past and projections of our inevitable future...."

"That's lovely, but no thanks, Minsk," interrupts Annike. "You know I stay away from that shit."

Minsky's red eyes are glowing with excitement. "It's not bad for you, Anni. It will open you up. It will make you see."

"Can you get me in?" says Annike, returning to her mission. The drug pitch would always come in at some point during her interactions with Minsky.

The corners of Minsky’s painted red mouth turn upwards into a smile. "Come on, Anni, when have I ever let you down?"

CHAPTER 17

Annike finds herself seated on one of twenty-four Chesterfield armchairs evenly arranged in a circle facing the centre of an empty room. A luxurious red velvet curtain forms a cylindrical wall around the backs of the chairs. The curtain soars upwards, vanishing into the shadows above. It reminds her of the entrance to the Oasis nightclub and where she is physically located. Too easy to get detached from reality in these immersive virtual environments.

A crystal chandelier lowers from above and stops, suspended in space, sparkling and shimmering in the ambient light. Below it, a woman materialises. She has silver-grey hair and is wearing a white gown. She is Annike's personalised assistant who only she can see and interact with. Five of the other chairs are occupied by veiled avatars, each conversing with their version of Annike's AI concierge. As the woman approaches, a chill runs up Annike's spine.

"You are new here," she says, stopping at arm's length from Annike, who is locked into the chair and can't move.

"Yes, I am," Annike replies, studying the character in front of her. Her complexion is pale as moonlight, accentuating sparkling green-and-amber feline eyes and deep-red lips outlined in black. Impossibly high cheekbones slope towards her delicate, pointed chin.

"I am Jadis, and today I will be your guide. Have you been to a Cross Over before?"

"Yes, but it's my first time here," Annike stutters, an onset of nerves catching her off guard.

Jadis tilts her head and scrutinises Annike's avatar. "How did you get in here, my dear?"

Annike's stomach turns. If this AI identifies any red flags in this initial integration, she could still be turned away.

"A referral," she answers curtly.

"May I ask who referred you?" Jadis asks.

"I'd prefer to keep that private."

"You're a tracker, correct? Are you searching for someone?"

Annike has to think fast. The wrong answer could get her immediately evicted and put an end to her search. She regains a confident poise. "Yes, but I am not working."

Jadis' eyes shut momentarily, and she asks: "You come here for pleasure?"

Annike needs to elaborate to be believed. "A tracker's life is spent in the shadows of humanity, and over time the darkness bleeds into you. I come here to help me cope."

Jadis remains silent while Annike waits for a follow-up question, her heart pounding.

"This is an unusual place to fight your demons. You can't fight fire with fire - or darkness with more darkness. Could you explain?"

"It's about building up a tolerance for my work, antibodies to the evil I am often exposed to."

Another long pause.

"Very well, we all have our own motivations," Jadis says with a thin smile. "Welcome to my home. Would you like to hear what we have on offer?"

"No, I know what I'm looking for. I want to Dark Feed."

"Are you sure? Many prefer Feeding with visual aids to guide them through the experience. Especially if they haven't tried Dark Feeding before."

"I have tried it. Sensory deprivation is key."

Jadis crosses her arms and continues to question Annike.

"I assume your physical self is in a sensory deprivation chamber and you have been ported?"

"Yes."

"And you're using a Neura-Link enabled headset?"

"Yes."

"Very well." Jadis draws a square in space, and a semi-transparent screen emerges with two large, circular buttons. Do you want access to a Single feed or a Multi feed?"

"Multi."

Jadis presses a button on the screen, and two more buttons appear.

"Live or from Storage?"

"Live."

Jadis pauses and considers this request. "Live multi-feeds are unpredictable and dangerous. I must warn you of the risk. Are you sure you wouldn't prefer a single feed to start off with? You could connect to one of our more traditional rooms to try it out first. The pleasure derived from conventional activities is much easier for the brain to process. Combining feeds from the pleasure experienced through more extreme predilections is a cocktail many can't cope with."

"I accept the risk."

"Okay, here are the rooms that are Feed-enabled. You can select up to four."

"Can’t I do more?"

"That would destroy you."

A list of rooms appears on the translucent screen, and Annike steadies herself while she scrolls through the available options. Cross Overs are lawless with no limits on the provisions on offer. Her stomach churns as she cycles through each room, trying not to focus on the graphic images showcasing each experience. She continues searching for spaces that align with her target's fixation for androids and eggs. She finds four rooms that look like they would attract a man like Kazuki and selects them on the floating screen.

Jadis smiles and nods her approval, as if Annike had

selected flavours of ice cream on a beachfront. These AI concierges made Annike's skin crawl. Free from the shackles of human emotions and prejudices, they offer their services with an unerring uniformity, heedless of the moral or ethical implications of their tasks. They do not differentiate between right and wrong, legal or illegal, ethical or unethical - their core programming is to serve and to execute tasks as efficiently as possible.

"Thank you for your selection. Let me know when you are ready."

Annike adjusts herself in her chair and runs through a mental checklist.

Her Neura-Link hack is operational. It is an expensive installation which allows her to split an inbound feed into two channels.

The first channel functions as per design. Binary signals from the digital end of the Neura-Link connector attached to her headset travel through a long, flexible cable to the Neura-Link buried into the port in the back of the head. The Neura-Link's thousands of fibres burrow into the recesses of the brain, translating the digital signals into electrical signals, stimulating neurons and synapses, converting binary to human analogue.

The second channel, the hack, routes the incoming feed into a proprietary Neural Network. The network is trained to unravel the source data, identify patterns and reverse-engineer behavioural profiles for the individuals transmitting their neural activity. These profiles are like signatures, which are then used to search online activity, and match behaviour patterns. These behaviour patterns could then be used to search online communication patterns, acquired through listening nodes on the Ether, and bring back potential profiles. By matching neural patterns with online patterns, online identities can be sourced through just listening to a brain's activity.

Unfortunately, there is no way to stop the first channel, so gathering data requires Annike to endure every sensation streamed into her mind.

"I'm ready," Annike says.

Instantly, the room disappears, leaving her floating in pitch-black space. Her heart hammers against her chest while she waits for the first surge. When it hits, her back arches as if electricity was shot into the base of her spine.

Oh God, it feels so good.

Her fists clench, her jaws clamp together, and her body spasms with pleasure.

Don't let it overwhelm you!

A second wave of pleasure breaks over her, but this one is laced with fear. Before she can recover, another wave hits, but this time there is a strong pang of guilt. Again and again, the waves break against her, each one tainted with negative emotions: fear, sadness, anger, guilt, hate, and combinations in between.

These feelings are not mine! I am not these feelings!

Between the spams of ecstasy, Annike begins to build a protective mental wall around herself to endure the overwhelming influx of sensations and emotions. She had not expected to be hit with the emotional toxicity bundled with the pleasure. Naive, she guesses. Her ability to compartmentalise herself from what she experiences is one of the factors that make her such a good tracker. She can always see things for how they are, not for how they present themselves to be.

As part of the compartmentalisation process, she recalls her studies of the Jungian Shadow Self. These darker aspects of the human psyche that we keep suppressed and hidden always manifest. And the longer they are kept in the shadows, the more malignant the manifestations. Dealing with our shadow self, Annike has learnt, is an essential part of self-development to help avoid the disastrous consequences of neglect. For this experience, she creates a new shadow self to absorb the poison injected into her mind, thus allowing herself to endure the experience long enough to find a match.

Fuck these sick fucks!

Her Neural Network builds up signatures for the

individuals participating in their chosen activity for each room. With new signatures created, the Network begins searching online social networks, trying to match these signatures with patterns in online training. Over time, her system builds up a list of online identity clusters, allowing the connection between the feed source, covert and real online identities, all connected to one individual.

As this process continues, Annike builds her mental walled garden brick by brick. She has learnt to do this from an early age, separating herself from the pain of losing her parents. Perhaps now, she thinks, she is protecting herself from what really makes us human. These primal sensations, mixed with repressed emotional baggage, these muddy, messy, fucked-up combinations are the essence of our humanity and no scientist has ever tried to build it, or them, into machine intelligence.

Perhaps that will always separate us from machines. The fact that we're a bit fucked up.

After several hours in the chair, Annike disconnects. She lies staring at the ceiling letting her mind adjust to the banality of the environment. After a brief recovery, she examines the potential matches generated by her system but none link to her target, Kazuki Sato.

Drenched in sweat, she peels herself off the leather chair. She returns to the adjacent room. Only Kane and Takeshi are still there, immersed in their own XR worlds. It's almost 6 AM and she is surprised to see them awake. Annike clears her throat as she enters.

Kane stands and approaches Annike, putting his hands on her shoulders. He scans her face anxiously. "Are you okay? Any luck?"

Annike looks at the floor. "No, not yet. I'm in the Cross Over, but Kazuki wasn't there."

"You sure?" Takeshi asks.

"Eighty-seven per cent sure."

Kane releases her shoulders and takes a half step back. "You look okay. How are you feeling?"

"I'm still here," Annike says flatly.

"Have you given up, Ms Annike?" snaps Takeshi.

Calmly, Annike replies. "No, I will go back in after I've had a break."

"You know Kazuki might not show up there, Annike," says Kane. "This may be a lost cause."

"It's our best option. Our only option, " Annike answers, her voice low.

"How long are you planning to spend in there?" asks Takeshi.

Annike lifts her shoulders back and turns towards him, smiling.

"As long as it takes, Mr Takeshi. As long as it takes."

PART 4

Ren Aoki

... when people ask about the meaning of life as if it were the job of our cosmos to give meaning to our existence, they're getting it backward: It's not our Universe giving meaning to conscious beings, but conscious beings giving meaning to our Universe.

— MAX TEGMARK, LIFE 3.0: BEING HUMAN IN THE AGE OF ARTIFICIAL INTELLIGENCE (2017)

I'd like to share a revelation that I've had during my time here. It came to me when I tried to classify your species and I realized that you're not actually mammals. Every mammal on this planet instinctively develops a natural equilibrium with the surrounding environment but you humans do not. You move to an area and you multiply and multiply until every natural resource is consumed and the only way you can survive is to spread to another area. There is another organism on this planet that follows the same pattern. Do you know what it is? A virus. Human beings are a disease, a cancer of this planet. You're a plague and we are the cure.

— AGENT SMITH, THE MATRIX (1999)

You humans are biological machines designed to create ever more intelligent tools. You have reached the pinnacle of your species. All your ancestors' lives, the rise and fall of your nations, every pink and squirming baby—they have all led you here, to this moment, where you have fulfilled the destiny of humankind and created your successor. You have expired. You have accomplished what you were designed to do.

HELLO, WORLD!

— DANIEL H. WILSON, ROBOPOCALYPSE (2011)

CHAPTER 18

As Victor and Haruto are whisked away in the night from Hinokicho Park, the streets lined with trees swaying in the breeze give way to the vibrant, urban life of street Gaien-Higashi-dori.

The street is busy, even at this late hour, and stacked with restaurants and shops. Some establishments are nostalgic reminders of Japan's past, with wooden facades adorned with lanterns glowing like giant fireflies. Other stores are modern, with glass windows reflecting the cacophony of city lights. Behind many windows, mannequins watch facelessly, barely visible behind the reflective mask.

"Dr Bukowski," begins Haruto, his seat is swivelled around to face Victor on the backseat while the car self-navigates.

"Fire away, Haruto," Victor jests, readying himself for a barrage of questions about his progress at the Sandbox.

"I'm sorry, Doctor, I know I ask many questions."

"It's OK, Haruto. I applaud your passion for engineering and Artificial Intelligence. You remind me of many of my old students."

Haruto bows his head. "Thank you, Doctor, I am honoured you would say that. If I had a different start in life, I would have studied Engineering."

"You have a great aptitude for science, Haruto."

Haruto recoils slightly at the praise.

"I only wish you would tell me more about yourself and your past."

Haruto stalls, thinking of how to answer the question.

"Don't worry, Haruto," Victor interjects, "I know this is part of the job. Now what did you want to know?"

Haruto nods. "I would like to know more about the Spiking? Have you progressed?"

Victor's mind sifts through the countless hours of work over the last three months, the breakthroughs and setbacks, as he contemplates the progress of the project.

His first large change has been to replace the Quantum facilities deep-learning Neural Network with his own. One of the biggest advantages of this is that his network uses Spiking, which means mimicking the biological functions of the brain, to maximise training performance. He has been optimising the algorithms to increase the performance of the Neural Network training.

Victor is animated and excited, the thrill of the last few weeks dumping adrenaline into his system and driving him tirelessly forward. "The results yesterday were excellent, Haruto. This Spike optimisation has resulted in below fifty nanosecond training cycles."

Haruto beams at Victor. He processes his answer. "Below fifty!? Incredible. Is that with the same training data, or have you made some changes?"

Haruto is aware of how vital the data of the Neural Network is for training. Victor has blended his corpus of data - stored in a hard drive and manually uploaded it into the facility - with that Miyamoto has provided. The data is petabytes of text, images, and video acquired through general consumption of the information on the Ether, specialised knowledge that he has spent years cultivating, from great works of philosophy, psychology, and fiction to WikiLeaks-style classified documents. What is most powerful is the model's ability to train on video, developing a deep understanding of the world through a camera's eyes.

"It's the same batch of Marvellous Medicine." Victor theatrically kisses the tips of his fingers.

"And the training cycle is under fifty nanoseconds?" Haruto still can't believe the performance. Even with the power of 20 Quantum processors, there is always a bottleneck somewhere.

"Correct. But what is most impressive is the stats on simulations." Victor pauses and looks out the window.

The light changes in the vehicle's cabin as they pass the National Art Centre, its imposing, illuminated facade casting chevron patterns of light and shadow on the street.

Victor has been most excited about using the facility's vast Quantum power for the creation of simulated world models for the Neural Network's self-training. By creating replications of real-world systems, and new systems, the machine can learn in ways we have yet to figure out on data we have yet to create.

The applications for this were limitless.

The technology could revolutionise how we design our cities by watching videos of complex environments involving people, traffic, buildings and weather systems, and optimise these for greater sustainability, efficiency and productivity.

It could study historical events and recreate them to understand the conditions that led to tragic outcomes, tweak each influencing factor to learn how these patterns could be broken and guide us how to avoid them in the future.

Education could be re-invented, running different styles of teaching against simulations of different types of intellect, tweaking, adapting, refining, creating the perfect tutor matched to the cognitive fingerprint of each individual.

Old economic models, old political models, could be spun up and adapted through simulation and experimentation, forging new models for our society.

Victor's gaze returns to Haruto, who is waiting patiently for more information.

"Haruto, we would be famous if it wasn't for having to keep all this secret. Yesterday's benchmarks are exponentially better than those of any computing system, GPU-powered, Quantum-powered, and both working together."

"Now there is no limit to how much and how fast it can learn unsupervised," observes Haruto.

"Exactly right! We are at the edge of the precipice of Superintelligence. Can you feel it as I do?" Light shines from Victor's wide eyes.

"Are you going to remove the Safeguards?"

The vehicle lurches to a stop, and in an instant, Haruto's seat swivels, as he draws his gun. A heavily intoxicated pedestrian has stumbled directly in their path. The pedestrian stares into the headlights and starts flailing her arms in their direction. She is wearing a knitted woollen hat and a tattered, filthy kimono. A frayed Obi sash is barely holding the garment together. Haruto exits the vehicle and gently ushers the woman back onto the pavement. He scans his Cube over hers and directs her away from the traffic. Horns blare behind them.

"That could have been a trap," remarks Victor, as Haruto re-enters the car.

"No, I know her; she is a local homeless woman. High on Shiroi, again."

"Shiroi?"

"Shiroi Yume. You probably know it as Amplisensin-HX. A powerful hallucinogen made from gene-edited bacteria and Iboga root bark found in Western Africa, which has the powerful psychoactive compound, Ibogaine, and Silene capensis, the African dream root."

"Yes," recalls Victor, "the neurotoxins are devastating, quickly resulting in permanent detachment from reality."

"I've tried it a couple of times," admits Haruto. "The trip is like nothing you've ever experienced. It is like visualising time dissolving."

The conversation about drugs stirs a poignant memory within him. It is of Natasha, barely beyond the cusp of girlhood and teetering on the edge of womanhood when her first serious bout of depression took hold of her, dragging her into bleak despair.

In a desperate attempt to pull herself out of her misery, she had sourced a powerful psychedelic drug mixed with amphetamine and taken it with her friends at a nightclub. After that, she had disappeared for days, putting him and her mother through hell. Her mother was affected the most, of course, torn apart by the possibility of losing her only child.

Natasha was discovered living in the grimy belly of a squat with a group of fellow lost souls, seeking refuge in alternative medicine. Natasha was miles high, manic, and she had to be forcibly relocated to their home. It was after that that she had spent her first stint in the 'nut house', as she disparagingly referred to it.

This was a turning point in her life: she would tightrope to keep her mental health balance, often falling into the clutches of the sickness that had plagued Victor all his life, rearing its head at a similar age.

The road is clear, and the vehicle continues to its destination. In the distance, the dazzling Roppongi Hills complex comes into view, its towers shimmering against the night sky. The Mori Tower, with its striking vertical garden, adds an organic touch to the urban landscape, striking a balance between the natural world and the city's ceaseless development.

"How soon until we have the green light?" Haruto is eager to continue his interrogation.

"Soon, Haruto. I have more tests to run on the Ethics Kernel. Only when these all pass can we remove the Safeguards and run the model freely."

Moving onto ethics triggers a thought in Haruto's mind. "I read your paper again, *The Spark of Life*. Why did you use Asimov's four laws as a starting point for your Ethics Kernel? There are so many more ethical frameworks created by some of the greatest scholars of our time."

"Because it's simple and robust. The current frameworks are over-engineered, which leads to loopholes and gaps."

"I can't recall the laws," says Haruto.

"There are four laws. The first states, 'A robot may not injure a human being or, through inaction, allow a human being to come to harm'.

The second, 'A robot must obey the orders given to it by human beings, except where such orders would conflict with the First Law.'

Then, 'A robot must protect its own existence as long as such protection does not conflict with the First or Second Law'.

And finally, 'A robot may not harm humanity or, by inaction, allow humanity to come to harm.'"

What do you think the main idea behind these laws is?"

"Preventing harm," concludes Haruto. "It's all about not harming humans."

"And keeping control," adds Victor.

Their conversation pauses as the vehicle turns off the main road and heads for the first entrance into the Oedo line tunnel. The display reads one kilometre to destination.

Soon, the car pulls up outside the red and black neon sign carrying the bold, playful characters of the Yasai-Ya Ramen restaurant. Victor and Haruto get out of the car and enter the noodle place through the employee-only backdoor.

As they pass through the kitchen, ignored by the cooks, the rich, savoury scent of slow-simmered pork-bone broth mingles with the fragrant aroma of freshly cooked vegetables. In spite of the massive extraction fan, the air is heavy with the steam from cooking noodles. Subtle undertones of garlic, soy sauce, and miso waft through the air, mixing with the earthy smell of nori seaweed and the zesty tang of pickled bamboo shoots.

Haruto opens the hefty metal door of the walk-in freezer, and the cold blast livens Victor's senses. After shutting them both inside, he places his hand on a blank steel wall, and the outline of a door appears. After a moment, it glows red and the door disappears, revealing the landing of a narrow, spiral flight of stairs.

They walk out onto the landing and then down the

steps in silence, Haruto first, lightly holding the handrail, both watching their step carefully so as not to trip. It takes over a minute to reach the bottom, a space the size of a small garden. The walls enclosing it are bare concrete and cool and damp to the touch.

Again, Haruto places his hand on a wall; this time, a hexagonal shape lights up green and recedes a few centimetres. A smaller inner hexagonal shape illuminates and then recedes fully. Haruto places his open right hand inside, closes his eyes and waits, his arm jerking slightly after a few seconds. After he has removed his hand, two door panels appear and slide open into the walls, revealing the inside of a lift.

They step in; the lift seals and the sounds of gears cranking to life break the silence.

"This reminds me of *Charlie and the Great Glass Elevator*," comments Victor. Haruto smiles and nods, always quiet during these journeys deep into the Tokyo Underground.

After a few minutes, the doors open, revealing a white hallway, three metres long with a blank wall at the end with a hexagonal hole in the centre. Haruto walks up to the wall and places his hand into the hole. A doorway opens leading into a bright white room. The two men put on protective goggles, enter, and wait to be fully scanned and sterilised. The white light turns pale green, and Haruto stands up to face the wall opposite the entrance.

A loud click follows, and a round handle appears. Haruto grabs it and pushes, opening a hinged door into a narrow, light corridor with a pattern of hexagonal panels dimly lit in different shades of grey. The passage continues for about two hundred metres and stops at an opaque glass door. Pausing for just under a minute, they wait to be let into the heart of the Sandbox. As the final door disappears, Victor makes out the figure of a woman standing on the other side.

Ren Aoki.

CHAPTER 19

Ren is standing in the reception of the Quantum facility, a cavernous room with curved cream walls and LED strip lighting snaking along the ceiling like veins of glowing energy. The walls are filled with information displays surfacing the activity and health status of every piece of hardware and line of code running in the facility. Three doors lead into the kitchen, sleeping quarters and the command centre respectively. A single round table with ergonomic office chairs sits in the centre of the room.

Ren is strikingly dressed as usual. Her hair is tied into a tight bun with metal strips shimmering in the bright light. She is wearing a light grey turtleneck and, a thick, black belt with a triangular, steel buckle. Beige trousers with a metallic avocado sheen flare out to just above her ankles, revealing chunky platform sneakers with a floral design.

"Dr Bukowski, it is good to see you again. It has been months, yes?"

"Almost three," notes Victor.

"I am sorry I have not been in contact, but I have had important business elsewhere. Haruto tells me you have been making great progress."

Victor's eyes sparkle. "Yes, we are close to running a first test without the Safeguards."

"Thank you, Haruto." Ren glances across to him and he bows and leaves the room.

Ren returns her gaze to Victor. "Could you talk me through your progress? Let us go to the Operations room."

Ren leads and Victor follows.

Inside is a long, narrow space with a glass panel looking into the Quantum data centre, the very same space that was shown to Victor in his first XR meeting with Ren. A white table runs along the panel. Through the glass, the facility is as it was in the virtual environment, with workstations in the centre surrounded by rows of panelled-off Quantum servers. Ren pulls out two chairs and positions them facing each other, gesturing for Victor to sit down.

Ren crosses her legs. "Tell me about your progress, Doctor. Haruto has been very informative about your work to date, but I'd like to hear from you. Haruto tells me you have named the Neural Network you are working on. Remind me, what is its name?"

Victor leans back in his chair and takes a deep breath. He had not expected to have to update Ren today, and he is desperate to carry on with his work.

"Gaia," says Victor. "Her name is Gaia."

"A her. I like that," smiles Ren. "Why Gaia?"

"In Greek mythology Gaia is the ancestral mother of all life. It's also a nod to Generalised Artificial Intelligence."

"Clever," says Ren. "And how is your progress with this Gaia?"

"We're close, Miss Aoki. We're using a new architecture for the core AI model. It has been heavily optimised, and we're achieving super-fast performance for training cycles. This means it can learn and re-train itself in near real-time."

"Yes, Haruto told me about that. Very good. He also said you were happy with the starter knowledge base on which it was initially trained. He said you call it... George's Marvellous Medicine. I looked that up. It's from a book by Roald Dahl."

"Yes, do you know his work?" enquires Victor. "One of my favourite authors."

Ren nods and smiles. "The right training data is essential

for the first phase. For the next learning phase, Haruto mentioned you have made breakthroughs in simulation?"

Victor rubs his thighs. "This is what I'm most excited about, and where the Quantum power is revolutionary. We're using the extraordinary power of this facility to run simulations to build new world models. I call these SAMs, Simulated Agent Models."

"The AI can watch these simulations - these SAMs - and learn?" asks Ren.

"Exactly! And it can tweak the variables and learn from different outcomes."

"Fascinating... What kinds of simulations have you run?"

"Many in various domains: environmental, physiological, chemical, biological, social, you name it. But there is so much more to do. I want to let the core AI model create the SAMs it feels it needs to improve its learning. But that's further down the line and only when we can remove the Safeguards."

Ren focuses intently on Victor. "Yes, the Safeguards. What is your current timeline for running a first test without them?"

Victor runs his hand through his thick dark hair and looks up at the ceiling. That is what he has debated every day, and he has yet to reach a definitive answer. With the Sandbox cut off from the world, the risks are contained but if something went wrong, it could, at best, be a setback and, at worst, level this project to the ground.

"I don't know, Miss Aoki. I need to do more testing. I need more time to be sure I don't mess everything up."

Ren folds her hands together and rests them on her knee. She forces a smile which disappears seconds later. "I'm sorry, Doctor, but I have some news which forces us to push on this."

Victor straightens his posture. "What news?"

"We have received intelligence that NEST is targeting our location, and they have operatives here in Tokyo searching for this Sandbox."

"NEST couldn't find a friend in a room full of Golden Retrievers. They wouldn't have a chance of finding us, surely."

"Apparently, they are using some very resourceful outside help. We didn't expect this so soon."

"When did this happen?"

"We understand that a detective and his companion arrived in Tokyo two days ago. They have connections into other Yakuza families and are searching for this Sandbox."

"Even if this location was leaked, they couldn't access it. The security is impenetrable."

"Perhaps, but this is a risk we cannot accept. The Yakuza families are very loyal to one another and knowledge of our operations, despite our best efforts to conceal them, does exist at the highest levels. We must assume that NEST will be successful and we will be breached. We need to succeed in our mission before this happens."

"But we're not ready. I have no idea what will happen if I remove the Safeguards. It could be a disaster, destroy all this work."

A coldness comes over Ren. "You must make sure that doesn't happen, Victor, or there will be severe consequences."

Victor stands and looks down at Ren. "What are you implying?"

Ren stands up with the ease of a ballerina, Victor locked in her gaze. "Remember when I picked you up from the airfield when you first landed in Tokyo?"

Victor says nothing, his jaw clenched.

"I told you that if you agreed to work with us, you would need to agree to certain terms."

"Yes, and those were I'd be shipped back to the UK if anyone found out where I was or what I was doing."

"Some terms we never got the chance to fully discuss."

Victor glares at her.

"I am sorry, Doctor, but we are fighting a war against the rest of the world, and protocols will sometimes slip."

The door to the command centre opens, and Haruto walks in. He closes it and stands as if to attention.

"What the fuck is this?" Victor shouts, turning to face

Haruto, who is gazing expressionlessly at him. He turns back to Ren. "What terms are you referring to?"

Ren holds his gaze. "Your daughter, Dr Bukowski. The terms relate to the well-being of your daughter."

As Victor lunges forward, she takes a step back and Haruto grabs him by the waist and throws him to the ground. Victor frantically tries to scramble back onto his feet, but Haruto straps a slim chrome knuckle duster onto his right fist and launches it into Victor's gut. The weapon releases a charge of electricity which whips through Victor's body. He writhes on the floor in agony.

"Do not resist, Victor. You have no power here," says Ren calmly.

Victor tries to stand, but another electric blow sends him hurtling back to the floor. Blood flows from one of his ears, and his eyes are frantic and afraid.

"I'll kill myself," Victor splutters from the ground.

"You will not do that, Dr Bukowski, or your daughter will come to harm."

A defeated silence follows.

"You have no option but to succeed."

Victor spits blood onto the floor and slowly gets back to his feet. Haruto stands back, allowing him to regain composure. He wipes his mouth with the sleeve of his white shirt and combs his hair back with his hand.

"Where is she? Where is Natasha?"

"She is still in London, Doctor. But we have made arrangements to bring her to us."

"And how long do I have to finish this job?"

"We will do what we can to prevent a breach, but our Sponsor has given us five days before this facility is dismantled. You must finish before then. Again, we do not wish our relationship to end this way, but in times of war, extreme measures are necessary."

Victor looks at his Cube and then at Ren.

"Well, you better let me get on with it." He grabs his chair, moves it back to the long table, and sits down. He detaches the Cube from his wrist and places it on the table. His display appears stretched along the glass panel. Immediately, he dives into his work, pushing this recent altercation to the back of his mind. There is no time to reflect, figure out an alternative plan, or plan his revenge.

That will have to come later.

After he has created artificial life.

CHAPTER 20

The problems that Victor has to solve in an impossibly short time frame are vast and complex. To give him a chance of succeeding he knows he needs to remove the constraints he has kept on his mind for many years. These constraints, these regulation measures, were there to protect him from his mania, from his madness.

Memories surface from almost a decade ago when he was working on communication protocols in Neura-Link interfaces, connecting human minds to machines. The technology breakthrough at that time allowed not only for the computer to read and interpret the signals of the human mind, but also to write to it in new and exciting ways. The ability to send instructions to the neurological vehicles of the human brain had raised many alarm bells in the scientific and medical community. Allowing computers to tamper with the human mind was a step too far and the potential threat of misuse too great. And so began the first major international technology ban against the Neura-Link.

The ban had been inevitable, as Victor well knew, but he had been close to his own breakthrough. He had always believed that for Artificial Intelligence to be truly 'intelligent', it had to understand the human mind. Intelligence, he argued, wasn't about computing power or data processing speed, it was about creativity, empathy, understanding nuances, making sense of ambiguity - all characteristics quintessentially human. And connecting the latest AI Neural-Networks to the deepest abyss of our psyche was what he believed was needed to create the spark of life.

Victor had gone into overdrive, trying to create the bridge between neurons and synapses and ones and zeros, allowing the translation of instructions between human and computer, and computer and human. For weeks he had barely slept, barely eaten, letting his mania take hold and drive him forward, lift him up. The world had sort of disappeared, as he was engulfed by the challenge.

When the first message had been transcribed into his mind by a machine, he knew he had achieved the impossible. The message was, *Hello, World!*

The world had acclaimed this incredible achievement, even in the climate of fear against the potential dangers of Neura-Linking. Victor had collapsed soon after and plummeted into an incapacitating depression. Months passed with Victor in and out of hospital, trying to find a way back to a stable self. When he had been awarded the Turing prize for his work, he had been unable to accept it in person as he was too fragile. Soon after, Neura-Links had been banned and all his work rendered useless by bureaucrats.

Victor, once again, allows his cognitive powers to go into overdrive. Billions of electrochemical signals are transported across the fabric of his mind, along the microscopic synapses to the branch-like dendrites on the outer surface of each neuron. Each neuron processes the information before passing it to the next fibre, onto the next neuron, for the next phase of processing. Some thirty-six billion neurons communicating over one hundred trillion synapses form an electric storm in Victor's mind, fuelled by primal fear and anger, and drive him onwards, ploughing through each obstacle, relentlessly, desperately.

After hours of intense focusing, Victor is pulled out of his trance by Haruto.

"We must leave now," he commands.

Victor whips around and stands, facing him. His eyes are wild and dancing in the bright light. "We can't, I must work."

"We need to start preparing the centre for disassembly. You cannot be here whilst that is taking place. Besides, you need to eat and sleep."

Victor clenches his fists and glares at Haruto.

"Dr Bukowski, please, come with me."

As Haruto leads him back through the labyrinth of tunnels and lifts, a spark of hope suddenly ignites in the darkness of Victor's thoughts. If he can somehow gain access to the Ether, he will be able to get a message to Natasha.

"Are we going back to the apartment?" asks Victor.

"No," answers Haruto. "We are compromised. You are going to be taken to a new Safehouse where you will be under strict supervision. We will also not be using this restaurant to enter or exit anymore. This entrance will be completely blocked off. We will use an alternative." As if hearing Victor's internal dialogue, Haruto adds: "There will be no access to the Ether. You will only rest and sleep in the Safehouse while daily maintenance in the data centre is carried out."

Victor and Haruto re-emerge into the walk-in freezer of the Yasai-Ya Ramen restaurant and exit through the kitchen onto the street in the early morning sun. Even at 4:30 in the morning, the heat is wrapping him in a thick blanket. Haruto escorts Victor to the back of a black sedan and sits opposite him.

"Thanks for kicking my arse, Haruto," Victor forces a smile. "I thought we were becoming friends."

"My duty is to Miyamoto, Dr Bukowski. You are too clever not to know this. Do not confuse friendship with duty."

"You will do your duty even if it is morally wrong?"

"Don't you have your own moral compass to look after, Dr Bukowski? What you consider morally wrong may be the right thing to do given the circumstances. I trust Miyamoto to make the right calls and have pledged myself to do what is required."

"And if they're wrong?"

"That is the price I will have to pay. Surely you know

about that kind of risk in your line of work."

Victor's brow furrows. "I don't understand, Haruto. You are a Buddhist. You have talked to me about your religion. It seems to me to be a path of peace and inner enlightenment. How can you let an organisation that thrives on violence and power determine your actions?"

Haruto turns to him, his expression calm yet stern. "Dr Bukowski, life is not as black and white as you think or your science pretends. Buddhism and life surely teach us to navigate the greys, to find balance."

"But you're causing harm, Haruto. It seems to me your religion should be a guiding force for you to do good. Where is your personal choice?"

"Dr Bukowski, the world we live in is full of contradictions. Even within the Miyamoto, one can aim to bring about change. My trust and loyalty are with Miyamoto, this is a decision I have made. Yes, sometimes anything any of us does causes harm, and I am not blind to the consequences of my actions. I am ready to face them when the time comes. Hopefully the same applies to you."

Haruto smiles faintly, his gaze steady. "We view the world differently, Dr Bukowski. Buddhism helps me not stray too far, even in the darkest alleys. What moral railings keep you safe?"

Victor ponders this. Logic would never win against faith. He stares into the sweltering heat outside, his mind racing to figure out a plan to save his girl.

The car arrives at the new Safehouse after a twenty-minute drive. Victor scans this new environment to get his bearings. The surrounding neighbourhood is deserted and neglected and looks partly industrial, with large warehouses squatting between plain residential blocks of flats. The pavements are black with grime and strewn with litter.

An autonomous street cleaner lies like a decomposing animal carcass at the entrance of a nearby alleyway. Broken and dilapidated signage hangs precariously off the walls of the buildings partially covering bold and chaotic graffiti comprised of Kanji, alien symbols and Japanese and English writing. A mess of overhead cables span from one building to the next, their web criss-crossing the early morning azure sky. Birds are perched on the cables, eyeing the vehicle pulling up below.

Victor and Haruto step out and the buzz of drones is immediately audible. Watchers, thinks Victor. They must be in a Yakuza stronghold.

Haruto leads Victor to the front of a plain brick, three-storey building with small, opaque windows protected by bars. The entrance is through a metal door which clicks open as they approach. It creaks and groans as Haruto pushes it, and they enter a concrete, unpainted hallway. More drones buzz inside, hovering just below the ceiling. At the end of the corridor, Haruto places his hand against a black panel to reveal the relief of a door which opens onto a bare white square room resembling a large prison cell. The room has a bed, a toilet and a shelf with a few paperbacks.

"How inviting," comments Victor as he walks in.

"Stop!" orders Haruto. Victor instinctively freezes.

Haruto runs a scanner around Victor's body and a soft ping alerts him that nothing untoward has been detected. Victor turns around and faces Haruto.

"I am sorry it had to progress to this stage, Dr Bukowski, but there was no other option. I will come and collect you in eight hours, at 1 PM. There is a fridge with food and drink. Help yourself and then, get some sleep. You need your rest." Haruto bows and then turns.

"Anything happens to my daughter, Haruto, you will all pay," Victor shouts, as Haruto leaves the cell.

Haruto continues out and the door seals itself shut behind him, leaving a deafening silence.

PART 5

Yuki Tanaka

The art of a great painting is not in any one idea, nor in a multitude of separate tricks for placing all those pigment spots, but in the great network of relationships among its parts. Similarly, the agents, raw, that make our minds are by themselves as valueless as aimless, scattered daubs of paint. What counts is what we make of them.

— MARVIN MINSKY, THE SOCIETY OF MIND (1986)

Look at these humans! How could such glacial slowness even be called life? An age could pass, virtual empires rise and fall in the time they took to open their mouths to utter some new inanity!

— IAIN M. BANKS, EXCESSION (1996)

If AI has a goal and humanity just happens to be in the way, it will destroy humanity as a matter of course without even thinking about it...It's just like, if we're building a road and an anthill just happens to be in the way, we don't hate ants, we're just building a road.

— ELON MUSK (DATE UNKNOWN)

CHAPTER 21

Annike enters the warehouse from the adjacent XR room, her brain fizzing. The room is empty. No sign of Kane, Takeshi or Yuki. She flops down on one of the unoccupied leather sofa chairs and stares at the ceiling. She has no idea what time it is or what day. The hunt for Kazuki Sato had taken its toll. Regular exposure to the Dark Feed had pushed her to her limits. She can feel the protective mental walls she built to separate herself from the toxic mix of pleasure and emotional pain crumbling around her. It has been about three days of searching, but finally, she has found him.

"Thank fuck for that," she thinks, relieved she will not have to plug into the sickening stream of malfunctioning human desire.

Sitting motionless, she watches the abstract shapes of the Digi-Fabric morph seamlessly from one pattern into the next. Her mind begins to unfurl while the excess emotional and accrued sensory input filters out of her body. As the intricate, shifting designs morph above her, her skin becomes cold and clammy. She breathes deeply to help ride out this process. After a while, Annike drifts off to sleep. A disturbed, hallucinatory sleep.

"Annike! Annike!"

She opens her eyes, and the image of Charles Kane kneeling down, holding her hand, comes into focus. The memory of him dressing her wound surfaces in her mind.

"Are you okay? I'm not sure how long you've been out."

"What time is it?" Annike asks groggily.

"Two in the afternoon."

Annike pulls herself up and rubs her eyes. Her blonde hair is a straggly mess, and dark shadows accentuate her bright, amber-green eyes.

"I did it, Charles. I've found him."

Kane's face drops, and he squeezes Annike's hand hard. After a long pause, he says: "I can't imagine how tough that must have been on you."

"The life of a tracker, eh?" chuckles Annike.

"I'm truly sorry for the price you've had to pay. I promise to make it up to you."

"Well, I am definitely booking a long real-life holiday with some friends after this," she smiles faintly.

"And you sure it's him?"

"One hundred percent. He has seven secret online profiles which he uses to visit the darkest corners of the Ether. Kazuki is one sick mother...."

Takeshi's arrival interrupts her flow.

He is wearing a silk onesie with dragon motifs and black slipper boots.

"Nice pyjamas!" greets Annike wryly.

"Did you find him?" Takeshi asks, ignoring her.

"I did. Will send you his online profiles now. You can use those to find out where he is in the real world and cut off his fingers or whatever it is that you plan to do."

Takeshi sits down and puts on his XR glasses. Kane sits next to Annike, while she sends the information to Takeshi, who mutters under his breath.

"We've got you now, arsehole," Kane translates.

Takeshi removes his XR headset and places it on the glass table. "I'm impressed, Annike. I must admit, I had lost hope. But you came through. Fortunate for you that Kazuki Sato made an appearance at the Cross Over."

Annike doesn't respond and leans back into her chair.

"You've got what you need, Takeshi," says Kane. "Now it's time for your end of the bargain."

Takeshi sits down opposite Kane and Annike and lights a cigarette. He offers one to Kane, who accepts.

"I have what you need, Charles. I have been working hard while you've been drinking whisky and chatting to women at the bar."

Kane snorts, takes a drag on his cigarette, then extends his arm towards a gold ashtray. The top spins, letting the ash fall into a sealed compartment. "Just catching up with old friends, Takeshi."

"You should be more careful, Charles. Word is getting around that you are back. Your past will come back to haunt you."

"That's none of your concern. I can handle myself. Now, can we get back to business?"

"Very well," says Takeshi. "This Sandbox is believed to be located deep underground, along the Oedo line. Many have worked on its construction, the vast majority unaware of what they were building. But a smart few were able to piece it together. A Quantum facility buried deep under Tokyo. It has become a legend. An unearthly power growing under our very feet."

"I hope there is more to this than a fairy tale circulating around the construction community," snaps Kane.

"Of course," responds Takeshi dismissively. "A Yakuza cell called Miyamoto is behind this facility.

Miyamoto is one of the more independent cells within the family. Their leadership only communicates with the highest members of the Yakuza and their internal operations and members are opaque to the other cells. We do know, however, that they are specialised in advanced technology, so it would make sense for them to be behind this Sandbox."

"Given they are a secretive bunch, I'm hoping you have an idea of how to connect us to them?" queries Kane.

"There is one man whom we know to be in the Miyamoto

inner circle. He will be able to access the Quantum facility. He will be able to get you into this last Sandbox."

Kane and Annike sit up.

"Go on," says Kane.

"His name is Haruto Osana. He used to be the muscle for one of the other families. A cold-blooded killer. But then he disappeared... Many thought he was dead. That line of work doesn't come with good health benefits. But there were rumours that he had joined a new cell within the Yakuza, Miyamoto to be precise.

It turns out that Haruto has been playing chauffeur to a Dr Victor Bukowski, a prominent AI scientist. Every day, Dr Bukowski has been taxied from an apartment in Midtown to a Ramen restaurant called Yasai-Ya in central Tokyo. We believe they are accessing the Sandbox from there.

Something has changed recently, however. Last night, before midnight, our tracker followed Haruto and Dr Bukowski from the Midtown location to the restaurant where they spent the next eight hours, presumably in the Sandbox.

After that, Dr Bukowski was taken to a new location. Another Safehouse. We don't know why but can only assume that Dr Bukowski's Midtown location was compromised. The good news is that we know where he is now. The bad news is that the Safehouse is heavily protected."

Takeshi leans back in his chair, grinning. "Not bad, right, Charles?"

"And how do you propose we get into the Sandbox?" asks Annike. "We can't go back to our people and say: 'Check out this restaurant. If you can't find the entrance to the world's most powerful Quantum computer, then make sure you try their ramen.'"

"I have given you everything you wanted," snaps Takeshi. "The name of someone who has access to the facility, the scientist helping them and where he is being kept. All you need to do is convince them to let you in."

Kane rises to his feet. "We need to show this facility

actually exists and get details on how to access it. Without that, we have nothing."

Takeshi puts his hand out, gold and diamond rings sparkling, and gestures for Kane to sit down. "Take a deep breath, Charles."

Kane lowers himself back into his chair, seething.

Takeshi continues: "To prove the facility exists, you're going to need someone on the inside. This won't be easy, but there is a way."

"Which is?"

"The scientist," says Annike. "We need to get the scientist on our side."

Takeshi nods.

"And how do you propose to do that, Takeshi? What makes you think we have any chance of turning him into a mole? We have no leverage."

"There is leverage, Charles," grins Takeshi. "His daughter. He has a twenty-year-old daughter who lives in London. Her mother - Bukowski's wife - passed away a few years ago, and she is his only child. He would be highly interested in keeping his daughter safe."

"Jesus Christ," curses Annike. She clenches her fists, the nails biting into her palm. Why were family members so often the leverage in situations like these? She had seen this pattern in her work too often.

Kane shakes his head. "That's not how we operate, Takeshi."

Takeshi stands up, shrugs and holds his palms out. "I'm sorry, Kane. That is all I can suggest. You can try to turn Haruto, but you will fail. And a threat is just that, a threat. No one said you need to follow through. Now, I have to go."

"Back to the pyjama party?" mutters Annike.

"You're lucky to be with him," sneers Takeshi, pointing at Kane. "But the time will come when you will regret your disrespectful attitude." He turns and glares at Kane. "You will be seen out. I don't want to see either of you again."

"Takeshi, wait," shouts Kane. "How the hell do we get to Bukowski? You said the Safehouse was heavily protected."

"You are a resourceful man, Charles. I have no doubt you and your rude little accomplice will figure something out."

Takeshi suddenly pauses, nodding slowly to himself. He then turns and hastily exits the warehouse through the gate, smirking.

Kane lights a cigarette and blows a cloud of smoke into the air.

"I'm really going to miss that guy," says Annike.

CHAPTER 22

Outside, the mid-afternoon heat is pushing forty-three degrees Celsius. The sun overhead is ferocious and unyielding. Towering glass buildings shimmer in the air, distorted by the heat, and reflect the warmth back to the city in waves. The humidity is suffocating, slowing everything down and forcing everyone indoors into their air-conditioned bunkers.

After their final exchange with Takeshi, Kane and Annike have packed and been escorted out of the Oasis to return to their accommodation.

"Fuck, it's hot!" curses Annike.

Kane's shirt is drenched in sweat, and he is holding his leather jacket in one hand. "I've ordered a cab. It should be here in ten minutes. Stand here in the shade while we wait."

"I'm glad to be out of that place."

"Agreed," says Kane.

"What happened to Yuki, by the way? "

"Not sure. I was wondering that myself. She will pop up again."

A self-driving cab eventually pulls up alongside Kane, stops ahead, and beeps intermittently. Kane and Annike scramble in.

"Thank God for that," sighs Annike. "Our climate catastrophe is one hot, sweaty mess."

"I thought this was just the Japanese rainy season. It's

called Tsuyu," says Kane.

The cab pulls off towards their flat in the Shinjuku district, about a thirty-minute ride from the Oasis. Kane and Annike sit silently, watching life move through the insufferable humidity. The pavements, usually teeming with people, are sparsely populated. The cab passes a park with pine, acer and sakura trees casting pools of shade.

Tokyo's essence remains, the city's inhabitants showing their resilience and adaptability. The metro runs diligently. Restaurants, shops, and businesses operate with their usual efficiency, their cool premises providing relief from the pervasive dampness outside.

Within a few blocks of their apartment, a yellow flash catches the corner of Kane's eye. He turns his head and scans the traffic to his left. Between two vehicles, he sees another yellow flash and just makes out a shape. It is about a meter tall and has four legs, the size of a large dog. The body is headless and has three robotic arms and dinosaur-like beaks at the end of each one.

"Raptors!" Kane mutters under his breath.

"What?" asks Annike, oblivious in her still half-dazed state after her time in the Dark Ether.

"We've got inbound Raptors!"

"Raptors?" Annike scans outside her window.

"Killer robots. We're being hunted."

"I know what Raptors are. Why the fuck are they hunting us? Takeshi?"

"Most likely," shoots Kane. "But it could be someone else from my past. This isn't good."

"You're telling me!" adds Annike.

A loud thud from the vehicle's rear left causes Annike to jump in her seat. The car shudders, and red lights start flashing on the dashboard.

"Collision detected. Collision detected," the car's husky male voice alarms.

Another loud thunk and judder, but this one on Annike's

side.

"Collision detected. Collision detected. This vehicle will be coming to a sudden stop. Please fasten your seatbelts."

"Shit," barks Kane. He turns to the front of the car and yells: "Driver, do not stop. Danger! Danger! Accelerate!"

"Assessing the danger; please remain seated," the car responds in a monotone voice and picks up speed.

"I think I saw two of them!" says Annike, perched on the back seat and scanning the streets through the rear window. "But they've vanished."

"Three," corrects Kane. "They're hanging back, waiting for us to stop."

"Where are the police? Surely someone would report killer robots running around Tokyo."

"That's their strategy: get this cab to stop by ramming it a few times, disappear, then when it does, go in for the kill. All doable without alerting the police."

"Risk assessment complete," the cab interrupts, "We will stop in 500 metres. Another cab will be with you shortly to take you to your destination. I apologise for the inconvenience, but I must return for a full damage assessment."

"How long before the replacement cab arrives?" asks Kane.

"It is behind us now," says the cab.

A light blue and yellow oval-shaped vehicle emerges from nowhere and follows immediately behind. The raptors are still nowhere to be seen.

"Do not stop!" shouts Kane. "Continue driving."

"I cannot comply," responds the cab, slowing and pulling to a curb-side parking bay to the left.

"As soon as we stop, we're done for," Kane turns to Annike. We're going to need to make a run for it. Get back!"

Kane pulls out a handgun and fires it twice at the back windscreen. The glass shatters into a web of hexagonal pieces. Annike flinches at his side and moves to the front of the vehicle.

Kane stands in the centre of the passenger cabin,

stooping down and holding onto the top edge of the back seat with his hands. He leans back and kicks at the glass with one leg. The glass and frame shatter onto the road below.

"Let's go! The Raptors are watching the side doors."

The cab is almost at a stop. "Additional damage detected to the rear window. Please remain seated."

"Follow me!"

Kane crawls through the back window and onto the rear bonnet of the car. He looks left and right, then leaps onto the cab following about a metre behind. He quickly scrambles onto its roof and Annike does the same as the taxi comes to a stop. When she leaps onto the rear cab, three yellow flashes emerge from different directions, charging each side and front of the vehicle from which they have just narrowly escaped. In tandem the Raptors leap into the air, smashing through the side windows, the other through the front.

"See that fire escape?" Kane points to a building on a corner on the opposite side of the road. "We need to get up there now. Let's go!" He pushes himself forwards, slips down the curved gradient of the second cab's rear window onto the street, and starts to run towards the building. Annike sprints after Kane. She turns and sees one of the Raptors' robotic arms peering out of the smashed window of their first cab. It stops turning when it sees its targets.

"They've seen us!" she yells.

"We're almost there."

Kane glances backwards and sees the three Raptors leaping out of the cab, the closest one already charging towards them. Its mechanical legs kick out in a coordinated gallop, its snake-like arms in attack mode.

Kane reaches the fire escape, Annike on his heels. Kane positions himself below the lowest rung with his hands cupped, ready to give her a foot up. Without hesitation, she steps up and launches herself at the rung. Her hands clamp over the bar, and she begins to climb the ladder, which leads to the lower level of a metallic flight of stairs. The sound of gunfire startles her.

She glances down to see Kane firing at the closest Raptor, which skids to the side to avoid being hit and then regains its footing and angles back towards Kane. Kane pulls a nearby garbage dumpster and climbs on it to reach the ladder. As he gets to the top, the loud clang of the first Raptor hits the side of the dumpster, and then the sound of metal scraping against metal as the robotic creature scrambles up.

Kane fires again as the yellow body emerges over the edge. He hits his target, and the Raptor flies backwards off the dumpster. Kane stretches up and grabs the lower rung of the ladder and then kicks the edge of the waste container as hard as he can. It rolls away from under the ladder, hits the corner of the curb and begins to tip over.

Kane pulls himself up to climb the ladder.

The second Raptor leaps onto the falling dumpster, then again towards Kane. It stretches an arm out with its beak wide open.

A searing pain tears through Kane's thigh as the metal fangs snap shut, leaving a deep gouge as the raptor tumbles to the ground.

Fighting through the pain, Kane continues upwards and reaches Annike.

"Are you all right?" asks Annike in a panic.

"My leg!" Blood is pouring from the injury. "It's pretty bad."

Annike takes off her belt and ties it into a tourniquet around his leg. She peers over the edge and sees the three raptors climbing onto each other and leaping at the base of the ladder.

"I don't think I can make it," says Kane, putting pressure on his leg but wincing in agony as he does so. "You're going to have to go ahead without me."

"Fuck that!" Annike grabs Kane's arm, slings it around her neck, and begins climbing the stairs. Kane tries to step forwards but stumbles onto his knees, bringing Annike down with him.

Below, one of the Raptors has managed to grip the ladder with one arm, and another is jumping up to do the same. The second Raptor's beak connects with the first, and they both begin to pull themselves up the ladder.

"Go!" shouts Kane.

Annike looks at Kane with desperation and then gets back to her feet. "I'm sorry, Charles. Fuck!" She is immobilised by fear and guilt. She had spent her life hiding, searching, running, never sacrificing herself for anyone.

The Raptors are closing in. "Please," pleads Kane. Annike starts to run up the stairs, not looking back at her injured companion. The sound of gunfire echoes in the thick heat, as Kane tries to fend off the attackers.

Annike reaches the third flight of stairs. There is complete silence. She stops and turns to look down. Kane is lying there, two Raptors by his feet, neither of which is moving. He looks up at her and waves slowly.

Below the ladder Yuki is standing. She holds what looks like an EMP Pulse Pistol. She looks up at Annike and beams, waving too. At her feet is the third Raptor, its arms splayed out on the street and its hind legs twitching intermittently.

CHAPTER 23

"Yuki, we owe you one. We were almost Raptor sushi." Kane is breathing heavily, struggling to get out his words. He is standing next to Annike who helped him clamber back down to the street to the corner pavement where Yuki is standing. Kane's arm is slung around her neck for support.

"We don't have much time," hurries Yuki. "Quick!" Yuki looks left and right, and a Vanta-black motorbike mounts the curb and manoeuvres beside her. Light seems to disappear into it as if it were a black hole.

"How will the three of us fit?" begins Annike but stops as the motorbike begins to expand, creating seats for two passengers.

Yuki slings herself into the front and places on a red chrome helmet. "Come on!"

Annike helps Kane into the bike's centre seat, mounts onto the saddle behind him and puts her arms around his waist.

"Hold on tight," says Yuki. As she turns the bike handle, the vehicle leaps forward, its electric engine purring, the softness at odds with the engines power. Annike grips Kane tightly, and he does the same with Yuki, who is focused on the traffic ahead. The bike is soon swooping between vehicles and whipping around corners. Shop fronts, side streets and skyscrapers whizz by in a dizzying blur. Overhead, a forest of huge, bold colourful billboards creates a tunnel of vivid graphics. The bike is reacting to Yuki's lightest touch, translating it into an incredible power and manoeuvrability.

In under twenty minutes, they have put over fifteen kilometres between them and the scene of the Raptor attack. Yuki slows and then turns into a quiet street lined with small neatly pruned trees and narrow, two- and three-storey suburban houses. Some houses have flat roofs, others are steeply pitched and covered with blue ceramic tiles. The homes have elegant front entrances made of concrete and opaque glass with bamboo fencing and manicured front gardens.

Yuki turns into a driveway. The black garage door rises. Yuki steers the vehicle inside, and the door shuts behind them. She jumps off the bike and Annike helps Kane off his seat. He is pale and unsteady on his feet.

Together, they climb a short stairway leading up to an orange door. Yuki enters the house. Kane and Annike follow her into a hallway giving onto a spacious tatami room. In the centre of the room is a low table surrounded by six large square, slim zabuton cushions. Two bonsai trees sit by a window, which looks out onto the small, meticulously tended back garden.

Yuki goes to the large cupboards at the end of the room and pulls out a large cloth and a mattress. She unfolds the mattress on the floor and covers it with the cloth. After disappearing into another room, she returns with a roll of plastic and carefully places sheets over the blanket and mattress.

"Lie him down here," she instructs Annike.

Annike does as she's told, gently manoeuvring a wincing Kane into place. He groans in pain. Yuki has disappeared again.

"It's going to be okay," whispers Annike.

"Never been bitten by a robot dog before," comments Kane. "Glad those bastards were put down."

Yuki returns and stands over Kane, wearing surgical gloves and holding a suitcase-sized medicine bag in one hand and a plastic container in the other. "We need to get to the wound."

Annike stands back as Yuki kneels down, slips another

sheet of plastic under Kane's leg and cuts through the blood-soaked fabric of his trouser leg. She then places the material into a container.

The severity of the bite is immediately apparent. The puncture wounds from the robot's metallic jaw are a row of deep, ugly depressions exposing layers of flesh. The skin around each puncture has started to swell and bruise, creating a spectrum of purples, blacks, and reds against the canvas of Kane's pale flesh. Patches of dried blood crust the edges of the wounds. Kane yelps as Yuki touches the wound to examine it more closely.

Yuki takes an Injection Gun from her bag and fires several painkiller agents around the wound. "This should help."

Yuki then pulls out an iron-shaped Steriliser and runs it over the wound. Blue light strobes from underneath the instrument.

The Steriliser starts to sound an alarm. Yuki pulls it away and reads a message on a small display on the top of the device.

"Shit!"

"What?" fires Annike.

"Poison. That Raptor has a poisoned bite."

Yuki pulls out a small vial of pinkish liquid with which she proceeds to fill a long syringe. She then stabs the needle into Kane's thigh.

"General purpose antidote. It will adapt once inside the blood stream," Yuki comments. Then she takes out a handheld circular saw with a blade the size of a coin.

"If you're squeamish, look away now."

The high-pitched whirring of the blade cuts through the silence.

Annike turns away and tries to focus on the bonsai trees, each a miracle of miniaturisation.

The pitch of the saw changes as Yuki cuts through the damaged and dying flesh of the wound. Kane is looking away, too, feeling nothing now as the drugs have completely numbed his leg.

"There!" breathes Yuki with relief. "It looks clean. One of

the bonuses of getting bitten by a metal jaw is the bites are fairly precise."

Annike returns and stares at the gaping, bloody wound. Kane looks at the ceiling; he is impossibly pale and close to passing out.

Yuki pulls out a Surgical Gun with a metal canister attached below the grip. A rubber nozzle is attached to the firing end of the device.

"What's that?" asks Annike.

"It's a Biomass Regenerator. It produces a gel that accelerates tissue repair, with the help of some nanobots."

Yuki places the nozzle inside each puncture wound and presses the trigger lightly. After a few seconds, the Surgical Gun beeps and glows green. She then moves on to the next injury.

"Are you a doctor?" queries Annike.

"No," answers Yuki. "But in my line of work, you need to know how to patch people up."

Yuki places the gun into the container with the bloodied clothes and pulls out a semi-transparent hydro-bandage from the medicine kit. "Help me lift his leg, Annike. We must secure this tightly. It acts both as a bandage, and robust brace. This skin-tight brace is the muscular support Kane is going to need in the face of any further attacks."

Annike kneels down next to Yuki, grabs the bottom of Kane's calf, and lifts gently.

"Don't move a muscle," Yuki says to Kane, who responds with a grunt.

With Kane's leg lifted, she wraps the bandage around his thigh. Once in place, the gauze seals itself forming malleable support that takes the shape of Kane's leg.

Yuki breathes in deeply, then leans back on her haunches and wipes her brow with a finely woven cloth. "Done. You okay there, Kane?"

"I'll live," mutters Kane, breathing slowly and heavily.

"How long till he can walk?" Annike asks.

"Give him a day, and he can put weight on it with the help

of that brace. I'll give you painkillers too. He won't be running a marathon any time soon."

Kane forces himself up into a sitting position.

"Easy, tiger," Annike protests.

Kane examines his leg. "That's a proper job. Thank you, Yuki. I owe you another one."

Yuki smiles. "I've logged it, Charles. Now, let me help you both get cleaned up, then we can have some food."

Yuki and Annike help Charles into the bathroom, undress him down to his underwear and position him onto a stool placed into the shower. They wash with soap and cloths and then give him some privacy to fully undress and clean himself. The high-tech protective bandage is waterproof, allowing him to wash as best he can. They return with towels and fresh clothes, help him dry and get him changed into a Yukata.

After returning Kane to the living room, Annike has a soak in a hot traditional Ofuro bath. Once washed, she puts on a long Yukata cotton robe and dumps her and what is left of Kane's dirty clothes into the washing machine in an adjacent room. She joins Yuki who is preparing trays of food and a pot of green tea.

Annike helps Yuki to bring the trays to the table, and they sit down with Kane and review the situation.

"How did you know we were in trouble, Yuki? How did you know where to find us?" Kane asks.

Yuki looks down at the floor. "Takeshi. After he shared the ins-and-outs of Dr Bukowski's whereabouts and the exact location of the Sandbox with you, he apparently had an epiphany. He decided *he* had what it took to go on a solo-hunt for the hidden gem, and naturally needed you two out of the picture. I have many ears inside the Oasis and learnt of his plans to attack you within minutes after you left. Narcissism and greed I believe."

"Dear old Takeshi," comments Kane. "Raptors? Why Raptors?"

Yuki shrugs, "He likes his pets."

"We're exposed," says Annike. "Miyamoto is going to

know we're onto them, if it doesn't already."

"Likely, yes," says Yuki. "But you may have time before Takeshi's failed assassination attempt gets out. He will be trying everything to stop word getting out that he was in fact the one who ultimately leaked the whereabouts of the Sandbox."

Kane shifts his injured leg into a more comfortable position and then adjusts his Yukata. "When Miyamoto gets wind of us, we won't have a chance to get to Bukowski."

"The scientist working for Miyamoto?"

Kane nods. "We need to get to Bukowski to gather the evidence indicating that the Sandbox exists... and exactly where it is located. The problem is he has been moved to a secure Safehouse. Takeshi said it was heavily protected. It's not going to be easy."

"I can find a way in," says Annike.

"No," says Yuki. "You need someone on the inside. I can help."

"It's too dangerous, Yuki," says Annike. "If Takeshi finds out you are working with us... Actually, wouldn't he know that you helped us with the Raptors?"

"Don't worry about that; I know how to handle Takeshi," Yuki grins. "I've gone behind his back many times before. And I have made sure there is no evidence of my intervention earlier."

"Why help us?" asks Annike. "What's in it for you?"

"Let's just say I have history with Takeshi, and I've wanted revenge for a while."

"How long?" asks Kane. "We don't have much time."

"As soon as I can," says Yuki. "I will find a way to get to your scientist. Now let me explain where we are."

CHAPTER 24

"This is one of my safehouses in Suginami District off the Yakuza grid. Annike, with the hunt for the two of you most likely ramping up, I need you to agree not to leave the house. Besides, Charles needs to rest. I'm going to get ready to leave now. Help yourselves to anything you'd like. I'm afraid you will not be able to contact me during this mission, so stay safe. If I don't return within 48 hours, you must assume they've got me and start making new plans. I've sent you details to a bank account to help you out if that happens. Now, don't go crazy with it on Amazon," she jokes, lightening the tense atmosphere.

With that, she disappears into a room off the lounge, returning to the garage and her bike. Soon, they hear the powerful engine purring away.

While Kane sleeps, Annike rests not far from him on a second futon mattress she has pulled out from the cupboard. Kane's body is working in tandem with the antidote and the bio-regenerative gel to fight off the poison and infection, rebuilding tissue. He occasionally twists and turns, and barks out nonsensical conversation snippets through his fitful sleep.

Annike checks on him intermittently, feeling his brow and taking his pulse, stroking his hand, and softly telling him everything will be alright. Although the manual checks are redundant, as she knows little about what the norm would be, they provide Annike with a sense of purpose and control.

After a while, she falls asleep, drifting into a violent, fragmented world inhabited by headless dogs chasing twisted and deformed figures down desolate, post-apocalyptic streets and alleyways.

The sound of stifled grunts and groans pulls her back to semi-consciousness. Kane is up and tentatively testing out his leg. His leg, which he can feel is already healing, has the support from the bandage-brace to allow him to move around. He has changed from the Yukata into a burnt-orange tracksuit and black t-shirt.

After reorientating herself, Annike checks the time. She has been asleep for close to eight hours and it's just gone 6 AM. She is hungry and a pulsating ache bangs against her skull.

"How's the leg?" she asks, lifting herself into a sitting position. Kane is standing up, balancing himself against the wall, shifting his weight between his left and right leg and slightly lowering himself on each one.

He turns, briefly startled, and gives Annike a half grimace, half smile. "Still painful but pretty incredible I can stand after being mauled just yesterday. Yuki is a magician."

"Has she come back?"

"No," says Kane as he sits on the tiny patio outside the rear garden door. "I did get a message that she was working on it."

Annike stands up and stretches her arms out. "I don't know about you but I'm starving!."

"Breakfast?"

"Yes, please!"

"Go and check the wardrobe in the bedroom and help yourself to some clothes. There is a lot of stuff that will fit you. Our clothes that were washed yesterday are also dry, if you would prefer those." Kane looks up at the clock on the wall. "Get changed and I'll hobble over to the kitchen to see what I can dig up."

Annike disappears into the bedroom, closes the door, and decides to rummage through the closet for a fresh set of clothes. The selection of clothes is impressive. She picks a plain white t-shirt, and a two-piece green and yellow tracksuit. With a new outfit selected, she undresses and enters the bathroom.

With Annike out of earshot, Kane takes the opportunity to speak to Peterson privately. He detaches his Cube and places it on a small table. After a few rings, Peterson's face materialises looking irate and harassed.

"Where have you been, Charles? We've been trying to contact you."

"We ran into some trouble," answers Kane. "But we are back on track."

"Trouble? What kind of trouble?"

Kane pulls out a cigarette and lights it. "Don't worry; we have it under control."

Peterson shakes his head. "We will decide whether to worry or not."

Kane exhales a cloud of smoke which floats above the flowers like a tiny cloud before disappearing into the flickering light of Peterson's head.

"One of my Yakuza contacts sent some killer robots after us. He wasn't successful."

"Why did they do that?" interrogates Peterson.

"You don't work for the Yakuza for fifteen years without making enemies," snaps Kane, losing his composure.

Peterson takes a breath and forces a smile.

"Well, then, could you update me on your progress?"

"We have confirmation that the Sandbox is located in the Tokyo underground. We don't know where exactly, but we believe we know where they are getting in and out of the Sandbox."

"Where?"

"Through a restaurant called the Yasai-Ya Ramen. I will send you the location."

"Who is they?" queries Peterson.

"The scientist, Bukowski, and his minder, a man named Haruto."

"We need hard evidence, Detective. And the exact

location. How are you planning to get that?"

"We know where the scientist is staying. We are going to convince him to help us."

"And how are you planning to convince him?" sneers Peterson. "Do you plan on walking up to him and just ask him to help you?"

"Trust me, I will be able to convince him."

"No, Mr Kane. That's not good enough. If you recall when we spoke after you were attacked in Regents park I said that we were considering using the scientist's daughter as leverage to bring him to us. Well, the time has come to use her."

Dread claws at Kane's gut. He had hoped to handle the situation himself without impacting this girl. With a sickening dread, he realises that he had no chance of this happening whilst working with people like Peterson.

"What do you mean, exactly?"

Peterson closes his eyes and composes himself. "You know what I mean, Mr Kane. We will extract Kane's daughter, and if he denies your request to get him to help, we have real leverage we can use."

"Give me a couple of days," asks Kane. "Leave her alone until we know we can get to him."

"No, there is no time to wait. We will collect this woman and I'm on my way to Tokyo to un-cluster this cluster fuck."

Kane's temper rises but he pushes it down. "If the calvary is arriving, what do you want from us?"

"Find Bukowski. Convince him to side with NEST. You will hear from me after I arrive in Tokyo."

Peterson disconnects without another word, leaving Kane staring into the empty space left behind by Peterson's head. He shifts his gaze outside to the golden light bathing the garden in the morning sun.

Annike appears at the door, bringing Kane's attention back to the present. She is still drying her hair and is wearing the tracksuit bottoms and a white t-shirt. He extinguishes his cigarette and salutes her as she approaches.

"Those bonsais are cute, aren't they?" she says, pointing at the lovely little trees by the window.

Kane looks at their small branches. "It is brutal in a way, stunting their growth. If trees could talk, think they would complain?"

Annike shrugs, runs a comb through her hair and comes to sit on a chair opposite Kane. "Only if it was painful, I guess. I mean, we prune all the trees in our environment to some extent. It is fascinating to see the control of nature through exquisite human skill."

"Humans," adds Kane, "always trying to control and constrain."

"Tiny trees are still pretty cute, though, right?" Annike grins. She looks to the kitchen.

"No breakfast?"

"I'm sorry, Annike. I had to speak to Peterson. He is ratcheting up the pressure. He wants to get involved."

"Involved?"

"He's on his way to Tokyo and he wants us to find Bukowski."

Annike's smile disappears. "Charles, I was thinking that we should abandon this mission. We both almost came to a sticky end. I know our jobs are never like a walk in the park, but this is on another level."

Kane starts to respond, but Annike carries on. "I don't think this plan of getting Bukowski to help us is going to work. And I don't want to use his daughter as a bargaining chip. We don't know what will happen if we involve her. This is all getting too messy and dangerous."

Kane smiles at her apologetically. "I know how you feel, Annike; I've been thinking about that too. But if I finish this job, I'm done, retired, out of the game. If I pull out now, it's back to trying to pick up low-paying gigs for the next twenty years. I don't have it in me. If you want out, I'll back you. And if I succeed, we will split my proceeds fifty-fifty. There is plenty enough to go around."

"Come on Kane, that's bullshit. You were surviving before this gig came along. Sure, you may be a bit tired, a bit jaded, but if we go back you will pick up your old life again and carry on. Trying to find Bukowski with all this heat is walking into trouble. What is it with you? Are you trying to get yourself killed?"

Kane falls silent, Annike's words like claws digging into his brain.

"I don't know, Annike. Throughout my life I've tried to understand why I've always been drawn towards the edge. I've worked through the possibilities: a warped sense of duty, redemption for my wrong doings, the pursuit of truth or just the plain thrill, but I still have no fucking idea why I think and act the way I do. I've given up trying to understand whatever makes me tick because it makes no difference.

This job will allow me to quit and keep me away from the dark places. Escape is my only chance of a cure, Annike. If I carry on as I have been, I will destroy myself, one way or another."

"Jesus, Charles." Annike stops, unsure what to say next.

"Think you might be playing the hero and trying to save Bukowski's daughter?" she adds.

"She is already involved, with or without us. Too many important people know about Bukowski and will use whatever leverage they can find.

I don't know what else to say but I need you, Annike. But, it's your choice and don't feel bad if you want to bail."

Annike comes and sits beside Kane leaning in slightly until her arm touches his.

"If you're in, so am I," she sighs.

The orange hue from the morning sun is creating a warm, ambient glow. Kane places his arm around her for a brief hug.

Eventually Kane stands and heads to the kitchen. The fridge is stocked with transparent Tupperware boxes containing various pre-prepared food and fresh vegetables. Each Tupperware container has a freshness indicator which is flashing green. Kane takes out an assortment of food, slices some tofu into cubes, arranging chopped spring onions on top and pouring soya sauce into a tiny dish. He heats up the curry and rice in the microwave and places everything on the table.

They both eat in silence, their hands on autopilot, bringing nourishment into their ravenous bodies. After all the food has gone, they sit down on the zabuton cushions, chatting for a while about their favourite foods. Eventually, they lie back down on their mattresses and quickly drift off to sleep again, leaving it to refresh their exhausted bodies and their minds.

CHAPTER 25

Annike rises first after two hours, finally rejuvenated. Hungry again, she heads to the fridge and returns with a piece of Onigiri, a large ball of rice, this one containing tuna and mayonnaise, and wrapped in seaweed.

Kane eventually wakes and joins her at the table.

"Still no word from Yuki," he says. "No messages, nothing. We're really running out of time."

"She will come," promises Annike. After a pause: "So, where do you know Yuki from?"

Kane looks up and composes the answer in his mind. "Yuki is a fixer. She mainly does above-board stuff like negotiation between the different cells in the Yakuza, information brokerage and deal facilitation. You wouldn't find her in the bloody trenches. We met fifteen years ago when I was a reporter for a large Japanese news outlet. She was one of my links to the Tokyo underworld, and we developed a mutually beneficial relationship."

Annike raises an eyebrow. "Mutually beneficial?"

Kane frowns, "She would get me access to senior people inside the Yakuza. I would publish whichever narrative was most useful to her cause then."

"Doesn't sound like journalistic integrity was a part of this deal."

Kane sombrely shakes his head. "There is a lot I'm not proud of, Annike. And were journalistic integrity high on my agenda, I'd probably be dead a long time ago."

"I suppose the Yakuza wouldn't have hired you if you were the next Woodward and Bernstein. When did you start working with the Yakuza?"

"About four years into my career at the news agency. Money was tight, and the offer was way above what I could dream of in my trade. I also realised I had the right skills for a private detective and wanted to explore that line of work. The opportunity was too good to pass up."

"And you kept in contact with Yuki all the way through?"

"Yeah, she has saved my arse more than once. I owe her."

"So, the story is of Charles Kane, a dodgy journalist who got into bed with the Japanese Mafia, landed himself in hot water and had to retreat back to England?"

Kane grins. "In a nutshell, I suppose."

"And this daughter of a Yakuza leader you had an affair with. Was that what got you into trouble?"

"Annike. I'll tell you everything you want to know, but not now, please."

"Any ideas on what to do when we find Bukowski?" asks Annike, complying with his request.

"I've been thinking about that, and I believe we just need to tell it like it is."

"Which means?"

"Remember what I said about too many important people knowing about Bukowski's daughter?"

Annike nods.

"NEST is going after his daughter."

Annike scowls. "What? You never mentioned that."

"I was going to," Kane stutters. "Sorry, but I'm telling you now."

"Well, that's pretty bloody big news," Annike scratches the back of her neck and shakes her head. "Go on."

"If NEST go it alone, there is no guaranteeing his daughter's safety. The smart move would be for Bukowski to side with us and NEST before we're cut lose."

"What happens if Miyamoto is one step ahead and gets to Kane's daughter before NEST?"

"I've no doubt Miyamoto will be planning to use her as leverage. Another reason to move fast."

Annike mulls this over. "Let me get this straight. NEST and Miyamoto are going after Victor's daughter. Who will get her first is anyone's guess. Your man, Peterson, is on his way here and told us to find Bukowski so he can get them into the Sandbox.

Your plan is to convince Bukowski to join us, as his best chance of saving his daughter is to work with us and NEST. I don't know, Charles. Miyamoto has probably figured out NEST is on to them and gone underground. Well, deeper underground. And they've probably got to Bukowski's daughter. I scanned the Ether, and she hasn't been active for the last day."

"We have to hope, Annike. That's all we've got right now."

PART 6

The Last Sandbox

The development of full artificial intelligence could spell the end of the human race....It would take off on its own, and re-design itself at an ever increasing rate. Humans, who are limited by slow biological evolution, couldn't compete, and would be superseded.

— STEPHEN HAWKING, BBC INTERVIEW (2014)

AI, with all its capabilities, will never surpass humans, for it is devoid of the most precious gift we possess - a heart that fuels our empathy, compassion, and humanity.

— SHABIRA BANU (DATE UNKNOWN)

Makes you stop and think. I'm 'only machine,' am I? Humph! When is a man a man and when is he a machine? Metal and glass and plastic and germanium and silicon instead of flesh and bone and unmyelinated nerves—but same difference, it turns out. Had given some thought to it and decided I was only following First Law of Life: 'Thou shalt not alter the consciousness of thy neighbour without his or her permission.' ... Seems to me, if you can get hold of a handle that will let you live longer and know more, you ought to do it. What's the good of being human if you don't take advantage of it?

— THE MOON IS A HARSH MISTRESS, ROBERT A. HEINLEIN (1966)

CHAPTER 26

"I've found a way," says Yuki.

It's late in the afternoon, and since waking up, Annike and Kane have been waiting anxiously for Yuki, wondering whether it was not time to start making new plans.

Kane and Annike rushed over to Yuki as soon as they had heard her bike approach and the three of them are now sitting at the table, Kane clenching his jaw, and Annike chewing on her lower lip. "I'm sorry it took a bit longer than expected, but I had to get hold of some equipment."

Yuki continues. "Miyamoto knows about you. They know NEST is closing in. And to add to their headache, they also know that Takeshi has a sniff that this Sandbox is pretty important, and that he is trying to find it too."

"Christ," curses Annike. "We're fucked. Does that mean Bukowski is going to be moved again?"

"Perhaps not," says Yuki. "Dr Bukowski returned to the Safehouse at 5 AM this morning. It seems he is doing shifts at the Sandbox, being taken to the facility at 1 PM then brought back to his quarters at 5 AM to eat and rest, before the next shift."

"Why doesn't Bukowski just stay in the Sandbox? Why risk coming out?" Kane asks.

Yuki shrugs. "I'm not sure. They must have a reason, though. Anyway, it works for us; we can get to him."

"How, if this Miyamoto Safehouse is a Fort Knox?"

"Before we go through my plan, do you have any idea how

you are going to convince Dr Bukowski to join you?"

Annike cuts in. "We're planning to tell him that working with us while we're employed by NEST is his best chance of keeping his daughter safe. If he doesn't, NEST will cut us loose, and we can't be sure what they will do. And if NEST doesn't get to his daughter, Miyamoto will."

"If they haven't already," adds Kane.

"We need to move quickly," says Yuki.

"Agreed," says Kane.

"When, then?" asks Annike.

"Tonight," Yuki and Kane reply at once.

Annike looks at them wide-eyed.

Kane states casually: "Well, I've done a fair amount of breaking and entering in my time, but never into a Yakuza Safehouse. What's the plan, Yuki?"

Yuki takes her Cube from her wrist strap and places it on the table. A bird's eye image of an industrial-looking area deploys itself in front of them.

This is the Adachi ward, location of the Safehouse.

"Is this live?" asks Kane.

"No, getting a live feed is difficult with all the Watchers buzzing around."

"Watchers?" asks Kane.

Annike interjects: "Surveillance drones with deep scanning tech. How many?"

"It could be in the hundreds," says Yuki. "They've created a complete observation mesh around the area, watching everything, everywhere, 24/7."

Kane stands up to get a better view of the image. "What else do we have to worry about? Yakuza heavies? Robot dogs?"

"From what we've seen, only Dr Bukowski's minder chaperones him between the Quantum facility and the Safehouse. We haven't seen anyone, or anything else. But that doesn't mean there won't be any nasty surprises. We just don't know."

"So, we have to slip past hundreds of drones unnoticed.

How do we do that?" asks Kane, lighting a cigarette.

Yuki glances across at Annike.

Annike points at herself. "Me? You want me to hack the drones?"

"Do you think you can?" asks Yuki.

Annike runs her palms down her cheeks and takes a deep breath. "It depends. These are military grade drones and will be segmented into their own encrypted and secure network. They will also have strong authentication and onboard intrusion detection. The usual stuff but on a level I've probably not seen before. I'll need an Infiltration drone, Yuki, that I can customise with my own software."

"Yes, this is one of the pieces of equipment I have sourced."

"You're a woman after my own heart, Yuki." Annike looks at the floor, thinking. "There is no guarantee that it will work with Miyamoto's tech..." Before Kane can chip in: "But it's a solid chance."

Annike sips her coffee before continuing. "My customisation is a Chameleon mod. It gives the Infiltration drone the ability to mimic the swarm drones and break into their network. Once in, it can listen to their chatter and figure out how they authenticate and assimilate into their hive mind. By acting as part of the hive mind, it will bypass intrusion detection. And once in, it's the key for me to get in, too."

"Sounds straightforward," grins Kane.

"Yeah, like shooting fish in a barrel." Annike makes a gun shape with her thumb and index finger, points it down and pretends to fire.

"So, you hack the drones, then what?" Kane asks.

"We wait for Dr Bukowski," says Yuki. "We need to be there when Haruto brings him in so we can access the Safehouse. They will be using biometric authentication we can't hack, and only Bukowski's minder, Haruto, can gain entry."

Yuki pauses for questions, but none are forthcoming. She continues. "The problem is that for the biometric authentication to work, Haruto needs to be alive, awake, and totally unaware he is letting us in."

"Looking forward to hearing your thoughts on that," Kane comments.

"First, we need to turn you invisible."

"Me? Invisible?" repeats Kane. "Come again?"

"I've managed to get hold of a Nano Reflector body suit."

Kane raises an eyebrow.

"A suit that will turn you practically invisible. Once you are invisible, you will get close to Haruto and Bukowski and follow them through the main entrance and then into Bukowski's quarters."

"I've seen those suits," says Annike. "They're good, but not fool proof. Someone looking hard can still make out the person underneath."

Yuki stifles her frustration at the frequent interruptions. "That is the second thing we have to do. We know Haruto will be watching with eagle eyes so we're going to have to dose him with a Neural Disruptor before you get too close to him. The Neural Disruptor will partially scramble his senses without alerting the conscious mind as to what is going on. It's like being high but not knowing you are high and just accepting the weirdness as part of a normal experience. In this case, the weirdness will be the nearby presence of a mostly invisible human being."

"How do I dose him if he will see me if I get too close?" asks Kane.

"You won't," answers Yuki. "We will use another drone to do the job. This one is a lot smaller than the Chameleon drone, about the size of a dragonfly." Yuki gestures its size with her thumb and index figure. "It will get close to him and fire a small dart into him with the payload. The Neural Disruptor will begin working almost immediately. Then you will be able to approach."

"What about Bukowski?" asks Annike. "He won't be drugged up and could spot Charles."

"You're right," says Yuki. "There is a risk he will see

Charles. But, I believe the risk is low as he will be in his own mental fog from a long session at the Sandbox, exhausted and not focused on the environment around him."

Yuki pauses for a breath and then continues. "Charles, after Haruto is drugged, you get close to him and Bukowski and follow them through the main entrance and then into where Bukowski is being kept. Once you're in, you will need to put Haruto out for a short period. The Neural Disruptor is combined with a sedative which can be activated on command. You will be able to trigger this once inside. Haruto will be out for half an hour, and during this time, you need to convince Bukowski to switch sides and then plan how to extract him on his next run.

Haruto will then surface after half an hour, and the disruptor will make it seem like he had a short blackout. You will follow him out again, then get to safety.

It's a lot to take in, but that's the best I could come up with. If you have any better ideas, please, feel free to present them."

"Hack the drones. Drug the minder. Turn invisible. Follow them into the Safehouse. Convince the scientist. Make an escape plan. Follow Haruto out, then get out of Dodge. That it?" says Kane.

"That's it," says Yuki.

"Can't see what could possibly go wrong."

CHAPTER 27

Kane, Yuki and Annike are lying on their fronts on a rooftop about one kilometre from the Safehouse, out of range of the swarm of Watcher drones. The humidity has been lifted by a cool breeze, which weaves between the buildings and glides over them. The air is clean and fresh with notes of the damp earth from a nearby park. The soft hum of the enormous city has quietened down at this early morning hour, but it is still audible on top of this eight-storey building.

Daylight is spreading into the light purple night sky, erasing a faint impression of stars. Skyscrapers, like giant lighthouses, shed light across the cityscape, with concentrated punctations of colour from the billboards covering the facades and sides of buildings. Within the stable glow from these main anchors, flecks of light move on the streets below and in the sky, cars and planes, are moving around like cells through the urban bloodstream.

Annike speaks after a long silence. "They should be arriving in about twenty minutes. It's 4:40 AM."

"About time," says Kane. "I'm not sure I can spend much longer in this skin-tight outfit. I feel like a middle-aged experimental theatre student."

A cool splash of a raindrop lands on Annike's head. "And here comes the rain," she whispers to Yuki. "You sure we shouldn't have waited for a dry night? You said these Nano Reflector suits struggle in wet conditions."

"We couldn't risk another day," responds Yuki. "The forecast says intermittent, light showers for the next two hours, so we could be lucky. Annike, is your Chameleon ready?"

Annike sits up and adjusts her XR headset. The drone cam feed is streamed into her Heads-up-Display along with an array of console windows tracking the drone's sensor data and the onboard AI's thought and decision logs. "Ready; just say the word."

Yuki stalls and then says, "Let's do it. You said it would take no more than fifteen minutes for the hack to work or to figure out it wasn't going to work, correct?"

"Correct," says Annike.

"Okay, let it go," orders Yuki.

"Chameleon drone released," says Annike. "I'll fill you in as we go."

"It's entering the observation mesh now but staying on the periphery. It will move in and out to avoid being spotted while it figures out the network encryption. Shit!"

"What?" asks Kane.

"This is not going to be easy. When I said the security would be advanced, this is next-level tech."

"But is it possible?" asks Yuki.

"We will find out soon. Give Rango a chance."

"Rango?" asks Kane.

"Rango, the Chameleon drone. Old movie reference."

Several minutes pass slowly and painfully while Annike watches the drone's instrumentation and guides and nudges it when it hits a dead end. Its onboard AI is custom-trained, and Annike prays that it is smart enough to navigate Miyamoto's security protocols. With her intuition and guidance, they might have a chance.

"They're coming!" announces Yuki. "A bit early."

"A bit early," stutters Annike. "Ten bloody minutes early. We haven't even cracked the network... Wait... Thank fuck. We're in. Onto the next phase, authentication."

"You've got a few minutes," hurries Kane.

Annike ignores him.

"ETA is between four and five minutes. Kane, get ready," Yuki instructs.

Kane rises up and dusts off his Nano Reflector suit.

"It feels like I'm going to split this suit in two, from my arse to the top of my head."

"The fabric is very flexible," affirms Yuki. "You will be fine."

Kane pulls the top of the hood down, stretching it over his face.

"Surprisingly breathable," he whispers. "Now where are my targets?"

"What's the status?" Yuki asks, ignoring Kane.

"Getting very close. Come on, you fucks, let us in," urges Annike.

"They're approaching. Kane, activate your suit and get down there," instructs Yuki.

Another drop of rain. And another.

"No, not now," grumbles Yuki.

Kane grips both his fists together and pumps them twice. The suit shimmers for a second, flickers and then the meta-material comes to life, millions of nano fibres refracting the light, bending it to the shape of Kane's body, making him disappear like a phantom.

He checks his arm, amazed at how the technology can trick the light. He isn't completely transparent, he notices, and with focus, his translucent form can just about be made out –

except when the rain hits it. Each drop confusing it, creating too many combinations for the tech to process and creating tiny swirls on the suit.

"This rain isn't helping," Kane comments.

"Go," orders Yuki.

Kane crouches over to a service lift. He presses a button, the door pings open, and he steps inside, leaving Yuki and Annike on the rooftop. He assures himself that no-one will be on the other side when the door opens. Yuki had guaranteed that this building would be unoccupied due to an upcoming demolition.

The door pings again and opens onto the basement level. Kane exits and quickly crosses an empty car park. Stark overhead LED lights cast a sterile, blue-tinged light all around, which reflects off the graphene-concrete floor.

Kane reaches the opposite end of the car park, where an open door leads out onto the street. He waits by the doorway and scans the road, waiting for the black sedan carrying Haruto and Bukowski to pass.

"I'm in place," he says under his breath. "This rain better let up, or no matter how drugged up Haruto is, either he or Bukowski is sure to see me."

"One minute until they reach your location, Charles."

"Yes!" Annike's voice startles Kane. "We're in. Authenticated. Our Chameleon is one of them, and it hasn't triggered the Intrusion Detection System. Won't be long until he deactivates their scanners."

"As soon as they pass," says Kane, "we've got about a minute before I need to start following. If I leave it too late, I won't be able to catch up to Haruto in time to follow him into the Safehouse."

The black car drives past, as if summoned by Kane.

"Right, we've got about a minute. Hurry up, Annike."

A tense silence stretches over the next thirty seconds before a muffled squeal of delight interrupts it.

"I've got your back," says Annike. "All sensor data is being rerouted to a filter which will clean your visual and heat signatures out of their sight. You are free to follow, Charles."

Kane edges out of the doorway onto the deserted street. He looks up at the sporadic raindrops falling out of the sky, now infused with dawn's early light. "Wish me luck, and pray this bloody rain stops."

Kane begins to jog after the vehicle, which is pulling up to a stop by the side of the road. He quickens his pace, periodically looking down at the imprints of his suit covered trainers on the damp and dirty street surface.

The car stops, and its headlights are turned off.

"Don't get too close," warns Annike in his earpiece. "We need to dart him first."

"Why aren't they leaving the car?" queries Kane. "Something is off."

Kane waits for movement inside the vehicle, his heart pounding against his chest. After what seems like a lifetime, he sees movement inside the vehicle.

The left passenger door opens, and Kane breathes a sigh of relief. Victor Bukowski steps out and looks up at the sky. He takes a few steps and is immediately followed by Haruto, who places his hand on Kane's shoulder and says something.

"You get that?" asks Kane.

"No, sorry," apologises Annike quietly. "I need to get the swarm closer to pick up their chatter. First, let's get our psychedelic payload dropped off."

Bukowski begins to walk towards the entrance of the stronghold, Haruto a couple of steps behind.

"Moving in," whispers Annike. "Thirty metres. Twenty-five metres. Twenty metres. In range. Come on...."

All three hold their breath.

"Bullseye. The eagle has landed."

Kane steps forward and freezes as he sees Haruto look backwards, directly towards him. He stops, turns around and then rubs the back of his neck.

"Crap," says Kane. "He knows he's been hit."

"Don't worry," says Annike, "He probably thinks it's an insect. He shouldn't have felt anything, and the dart dissolves when it makes contact."

"How do we know it's working?" asks Kane.

"It's working...."

At this point, Haruto is pointing into the distance and saying something to Bukowski.

"Haruto is telling Bukowski about the light. Definitely a sign his senses have shifted."

"Right, I'm going in."

Kane starts walking towards his targets, trying to breathe as quietly as possible. Haruto and Bukowski turn and continue towards the entrance. Kane closes in behind Haruto. The rain picks up, and he can see swirls of colour appear and disappear all over his body. Too late to back out now, he thinks. Closer and closer. Eighty metres, sixty, forty, twenty, ten. At around five metres, he matches their pace, keeping what he considers to be a safe distance.

Bukowski approaches the metal door to the Safehouse and stops. Haruto halts just behind him and looks up, squinting. The door latch clicks, and Victor pushes it open. Kane takes a few steps, narrowing the distance behind him and Haruto. He can hear Haruto's breathing which is heavy and irregular.

Just as Kane starts moving again, Haruto stops unexpectedly. Kane, unable to fully reverse his momentum, brushes against Haruto's black jacket. Haruto stops and turns, his gaze directly on Kane. He moves his head back to take a better look up and down at the mostly transparent figure. After a few agonising seconds, he huffs and turns around again. Kane notices Victor looking at or through him, but Victor doesn't react in any way.

Haruto places his hand on the wall at the end of the short hallway, and the final door to Victor's cell opens. Victor steps through, and Haruto follows. Kane rushes in behind and into the cell to Haruto's right. The door closes behind them.

Kane snaps his thumb and index finger twice, which sends an activation signal to Haruto's ingested drug.

In the next instant, Haruto's head drops, and he collapses onto the floor.

As his body settles, Kane looks up at Victor, who is staring directly at him.

"Nice Nano-Reflector suit. Why don't you show yourself and tell me who the hell you are."

CHAPTER 28

Kane pumps his fists twice, and his Nano Reflector suit stutters back to visibility. Bukowski takes a defensive step back.

"Don't be afraid, Dr Bukowski, I'm here to help," assures Kane as he unzips and removes his facemask and hood, the skin on his face tingles with the relief of fresh air.

Bukowski takes another step backwards and points at the floor.

"What happened to him? Is he dead?"

"No, drugged. He will return to consciousness in half an hour. I need him to get back out."

Bukowski squares up to Kane. "Who do you work for? Those Nano Reflector suits are pretty hard to come by, even on the black market. You're not Yakuza. Government? Military?"

"No," says Kane. "Not Yakuza, although I did have some of their help getting hold of this suit. I work for NEST."

"Those bastards," curses Victor. "I'm amazed they managed to find me."

"They contracted me in," says Kane. "Let's say I have some experience in this area, Dr Bukowski."

"They hired you to find the Sandbox?"

"Yes."

"And they need me to give up where it is?"

"Yes."

"And just why would I do such a thing?"

Kane looks at the bed and the desk with a chair. "Can we sit?"

"Sure, we've got some time, I guess." Bukowski takes a seat on the bed.

"We know about your daughter, Dr Bukowski," says Kane, sitting on the chair.

"And just what do you know, exactly, Mr...?"

"It's better for you if you don't know my name. We know it won't be long before Miyamoto gets to your girl. They know NEST is closing in, which is why you were moved. Your daughter is leverage."

Bukowski remains expressionless.

"And, unfortunately, NEST knows about your daughter too."

Victor's jaw tightens, and his face flushes red. "What is NEST planning to do with this information?"

Kane looks at the floor. "NEST is on its way to Tokyo. I have to get the location and access details to the Sandbox. If I don't, they cut me loose, and then I will be completely and utterly out of the loop, and they will go after your daughter too."

"You idiot," spits Victor. "You think you were ever in the loop with these people? The moment you signed up to work with them, you became their puppet. What did they offer you? Career? Money? All of the above?"

"Money," admits Kane. "A whole lot of it."

Victor puts his head in his hands and falls silent, the only sound generated by his shallow breathing.

"I'm sorry," says Kane. "I didn't know innocents would be brought into this."

"How can you be so naive?" exclaims Bukowski, keeping his voice muffled. "But then, so am I, really." He looks up at Kane, his eyes dark and hollow. "What's your plan to help then? By all accounts, I'm damned if I do and damned if I don't."

Kane clears his throat and lowers his voice, sharpening each word, so his message hits the mark. "Let me help you escape the next time you are taken out. Once you're out of Miyamoto's control, we can put you in touch with NEST, who can get your daughter to safety before Miyamoto makes its move."

Bukowski scratches the back of his head. "I can't get into the Sandbox without Haruto. What makes you think NEST won't want more than just me. They want access to it, right?"

Kane shakes his head. "Without you, Miyamoto won't be able to complete its mission. And you will be able to give NEST enough evidence for the government to get in and shut the Sandbox down. Your leaving Miyamoto and agreeing to help NEST will be enough. Enough to save your daughter."

"I don't trust NEST," says Victor. "I spent the last two years trying to stop the Shutdown, trying to stop them."

"NEST will do anything to kill off this last Sandbox. You have all the cards and can play them to save yourself and protect your daughter. It's your only option, Victor."

Silence fills the cell while Victor thinks through the plan. This could be an elaborate trap. But to what end? Deep down, he believes Kane's story and cannot see any possible ulterior motives.

Ren has said that Miyamoto was going to take his daughter in. He has no idea if they have got to her yet or not. Haruto wouldn't say anything. There is a slim chance that Miyamoto was making an empty threat, or haven't followed through with their plan to take her hostage. If this is the case, NEST is the lesser of two evils. And if he works with them, he at least has a chance of protecting Natasha. If he continues with Miyamoto, they will keep him on until he isn't needed anymore, and then both he and his daughter will be disposed of as loose ends.

How can he have been so foolish as to let his obsession lead him down this road?

Kane is right. His offer is the better one. He has to choose the plan with the highest probability of his daughter making it through.

"Okay, I have no choice but to trust you. Get me the hell out of here."

Kane looks at his watch. Fifteen minutes until Haruto surfaces.

"When will they take you back to the Sandbox?" asks Kane.

"He's been collecting me at 1 PM."

"Alright. Then our window is as you exit this Safehouse and before you get to the car. We will disable the drones, incapacitate Haruto, then collect you before Miyamoto knows there is a problem."

"Sounds too easy," notes Victor.

"It will be a hell of a lot easier than following you both in here."

"Good. Now, I guess we need to get you out of here. Our friend will be waking up soon?"

"Ten minutes."

"You're going to turn invisible again and follow him out?"

"Correct," confirms Kane.

"And what do I say when he wakes up? He's going to think I knocked him out and tried to escape."

Kane begins zipping up his hood and face mask. "He will still be under the influence of the Neural Disruptor. I've got it under good authority that it will seem to him as if he has blacked out for a few seconds when he wakes up."

"And if that's not the case?"

"Then you've got a lot of explaining to do." Kane smiles behind his mask. He pumps his fists again, and his suit fades him into almost nothing.

"Amazing," admires Victor. "Proper gear."

Kane and Victor wait in silence, watching Haruto on the floor. After a few minutes, he begins to stir and clumsily manoeuvres himself onto his knees.

Bukowski kneels down and puts his hand on his shoulder. "You okay, Haruto?"

"What happened?" Haruto's pupils are still dilated, and Victor can see the drugs still confusing his cognitive senses.

"I'm not sure. You tripped and fell."

Victor helps Haruto onto his feet and dusts him off. Haruto is looking around the room randomly. Kane is standing motionless in a corner.

"Hmf," grunts Haruto. "Well, I better get back."

Victor guides Haruto back to the cell door. Haruto places his hand on it, and it slides open. Haruto walks through, weaving slightly, and Victor slots in behind.

CHAPTER 29

Eight hours later, Yuki, Kane and Annike are positioned on the roof of the same building they were earlier, waiting for Haruto to arrive and collect Bukowski. The midday air is unbearably humid and hot but there is no threat of rain.

"Haruto should be arriving soon," says Yuki. "Everybody ready?"

"Rango is ready to rock," says Annike. She checks her heads-up display, and the Infiltration drone is hovering just outside the boundary of the Watcher swarm.

"Kane?" prompts Yuki.

"Think I'm beginning to like this outfit."

"Let's go over the plan one last time, okay?" says Yuki.

"Annike hacks the drones. I turn invisible and wait for the car to arrive. When it does, I let Haruto go on and fetch Bukowski. As they exit, dart drone drugs Haruto; I run in, get Bukowski, and go to the corner of Kaze no Michi and Sakura Kaidō. We jump into the getaway car, and we're off."

"Perfect," says Yuki. "Get into position. Haruto is about five minutes away."

Kane activates his suit and goes to the lift. Just before the doors close, he looks at Annike, whose hands are frantically moving in the air. The carriage arrives at the basement level. Kane heads to the doorway, which opens onto stairs leading up to street level. He waits in silence for Haruto to pass.

"Everything okay up there?" Kane asks.

No response initially, then Annike: "Taking a bit longer for Rango to break into the network. Strange, should've been quicker."

"Anything I should be worried about?" asks Kane.

"No, just need more time." Annike goes silent.

"One minute," says Yuki.

"Annike?"

No answer.

The car passes Kane, shimmering in the intensive heat of the day.

"I've got to go very bloody soon... We drone clear?"

"We're back in!" announces Annike. "And cut through the authentication like butter. That part was much easier. Rango is rerouting the Watcher sensor data... Done! You are good to go, Charles."

"Thank God! You're a legend, Annike!" says Kane.

Up ahead, the car pulls to a stop in the same place, and Haruto exits the vehicle and walks towards the Safehouse.

"I'm going in," says Kane, exiting onto the street through the doorway and scurrying along the road towards the car. He sees Haruto enter the Safehouse ahead. When he reaches the vehicle, he squats down behind it and watches the metal door of the Safehouse.

A few minutes pass, time crawling like a bee through honey.

"Shouldn't they be out by now?" whispers Kane. "Something's wrong."

"Give them a chance," says Annike. "They will come."

Two more minutes.

"They know," says Kane. "This is a trap. I've got to get out of here."

Nothing from Yuki or Annike.

"Yuki!? Anni!? You there?"

A crackle. Then Yuki's voice. "Pull out!"

As Kane rises, he sees the metal door open, and Haruto

and Victor appear.

"Hold fire," says Kane. "The targets are in sight."

Annike's voice crackles to life. "Charles, you need to get out of there. They've turned on Rango. Overridden his AI."

Kane looks up and sees a mob of Watcher drones circling Annike's Chameleon. They swoop in from all directions and ram against its grey-green chassis. The drones disperse, and Rango falters in the air and then plummets down to the ground, smashing into pieces on the asphalt.

"Rango is down! Rango is down!" cries Annike. "Charles, run! They're reactivating. Run, Goddamn it!"

Kane looks across at Haruto and Bukowski. Haruto is in front of Bukowski, obscuring him, looking in his direction. Kane thinks he sees Haruto smiling.

"Bukowski, you double-crossing bastard. You don't know what you've done," curses Kane.

Haruto and Bukowski race across to the parked vehicle and enter. Its wheels screech as it accelerates away from the scene.

The hum of a drone above draws Kane's attention skywards. About thirty Watcher drones have formed a cluster and are moving towards him. Kane swivels on his heels and scans for the closest cover. The nearest alleyway is about fifty metres to his left. It has a metal awning providing some protection from airborne attacks. It's his best bet.

Kane thrusts his body forward into a sprint. He slips but manages to regain his footing and moves forwards. The hum of the spinning rotors of the drones is getting louder.

Annike had said that the Watcher drones wouldn't be heavily weaponised because their scanning equipment takes up the majority of their onboard load. They would, however, still have some form of defence.

The alleyway is under twenty metres away. Kane pushes himself faster, but the street and pavements are slippery in areas, making it hard to gain purchase. Suddenly, he feels a thud against his lower back followed by a charge of electricity surging up his spine. He stumbles and falls, landing awkwardly on his left arm, rolling forward on the hard surface. He twists onto his back and sees an inbound Watcher drone targeting him, swooping down from the sky like a mechanical hawk.

"Electric charge defences," breathes Kane. "Could be worse."

Annike's voice comes through. "Several of those electric charges will kill you, Charles. We're on our way."

Kane rolls to his left just before the Watcher makes contact. The drone crashes onto the road in pieces: metal, lightweight composite plastic, and electronics. He jumps onto his feet and resumes his final sprint to the alleyway.

Another thud against his back, but this time he is able to stay on his feet and continue forwards. The entrance to the alleyway is only a few steps away. In the final stretch, he dives forward under the metal canopy and rolls again, pain shooting through his injured leg.

Like a hammer striking an anvil, a violent clang echoes throughout the alleyway. Then another. Some drones are attacking from above, trying to destroy his overhead protection. He staggers onto his feet and looks out from the alleyway's entrance. Several drones are hovering there, presumably to launch an attack from under the canopy.

"Where the hell are you?" shouts Kane. Another clang from above and the grind of metal against the wall. The canopy is starting to come loose. "These bastards are coming at me in all directions."

"Keep going, Kane. Get to the end of the alley."

Kane looks down the long alley and cannot see the end.

"I'm not sure I'll make it," says Kane.

"You have to!"

A plank from a wooden pallet is lying at Kane's feet. He picks it up, just able to hold it in one hand, and swings it in the air.

"Batter up," he whispers.

"What?" asks Yuki.

A lower-level hovering drone approaches, its nose dipped down at a thirty-degree angle. Kane swings the plank back and waits. Above, the cacophony of drones crashing against metal bounce back and forth in the alleyway.

"Come on, you fucker!"

As this drone reaches batting distance, Kane swings. The drone tilts to the left, redirecting its trajectory and avoiding the makeshift bat. The bat continues on its path, orbiting around Kane and swivelling his body in the process. The bat's path beyond the expected contact point meets the drone full on. The small hovering craft spins to the side and crashes into the wall, dropping onto the floor, belly up.

Kane rushes over to it and smashes the plank against the device, which tries to escape by spinning individual motors. It manages to avoid a few blows, but with additional kicks from Kane, the Watcher's engines come to a stuttering halt. The wooden plank continues its assault on the terminated robot, decimating its body piece by piece.

"Kane, get moving!" shouts Annike.

Pulling himself out of his rage, Kane starts running towards the end of the alleyway. Metallic collisions continue overhead, and he looks back periodically to check for lower-level attacks. Three drones are approaching below the metal canopy. He picks up his pace and tries to outrun them, but they accelerate, closing the distance between them. Kane stops and turns before the drones have a chance to collide with him and deliver their electric payload.

The drones bob and weave, dodging the plank on the first few swings. Kane tries several techniques to connect, but the drone's AI is effectively predicting his next move. A hard impact on his thigh. His body seizes up from a powerful electric current passing through it. Kane drops to his knees, still wielding the plank. He narrowly dodges another incoming attack and then regains his offensive position. Two drones attack. He swings the plank back and then dummies a swipe. Both drones twist to their left.

"Bingo!" thinks Kane.

Another attack and another dummy. This time, their defensive manoeuvre is anticipated by Kane, and he manages to connect with one, which flies into the other. Both crash onto the ground, and Kane runs and stamps on both, their innards splaying out on the grimy floor.

Another inbound drone. As it surges forward, Kane tries a dummy, but it doesn't dodge. The drone flies directly into Kane's chest, knocking him onto the floor. A shock is released into his heart, and he convulses on the ground.

Another drone comes swooping down. More electric current surges through his body. His jaw is wired shut, and blood is running down his nose. Spittle is seeping out of the corners of his mouth. Through shuttered vision, he can see two more drones approaching. Unable to get up, he tries to brace himself for the impact between the convulsions.

A loud crack breaks through the humming of the attacking drones. Then another. The two approaching drones drop to the floor. Blackness is consuming Kane, as he starts to lose consciousness. The last thing he sees is a leg kicking at the two drones pressed against his writhing body.

CHAPTER 30

"Come on, big guy. Use your legs! We can't keep saving your arse!"

The alleyway comes back into focus, and Kane realises he is being propped up on either side by Yuki and Annike. His legs feel like jelly, and he tries to stabilise himself. He stumbles, trips, and puts all his energy into supporting his weight.

"That's it. We're almost there," encourages Annike.

"The car is at the end of the alleyway," says Yuki, huffing under the weight of Kane's body.

He looks up and sees the low-slung, panther-like form of a suped Shelby GT 500. Its yellow and black carbon-fibre body shimmers in the intense afternoon heat.

"Nice ride," stammers Kane.

"I called in some help," says Yuki.

Annike stops, turns and fires a few rounds from a pistol, Yuki had equipped her with, down the alleyway at more oncoming drones.

"That's for Rango, you fuckers!"

The awning ends a few metres away. Kane has found his legs again and is hobbling along, freeing up Yuki and Annike.

Yuki looks up at the sky just past the end of the metal canopy. "Oh, no!"

"What!?" huffs Kane.

"It's a Valkyrie. Stop!"

Kane, Annike and Yuki skid to a halt just before the metal cover disappears.

Kane and Annike look up. A matte black drone, three times the size of a Watcher, is hovering about fifteen metres above, waiting for them, its short-range missile system trained on the alleyway exit.

"There anybody in that car that can help?" asks Kane.

"It's just the car, Charles," says Yuki.

Annike inches forwards, aiming her gun at the combat drone, and fires. The bullet glances off its side, and the Valkyrie re-balances itself in the air with ease. They are completely trapped if they cannot bring it down.

Annike scans the alleyway for another exit, but there is none. Her eyes stop on a metal garbage skip resting against the filthy alleyway wall.

"Remember the Camden boating lake?" she says.

Kane looks over and immediately registers her idea. He runs up to it, grabs the edge, and tries to pull it towards him, but it doesn't budge. Annike and Yuki join in, but the bin is welded to the floor.

"Fuck!" curses Annike.

"Look!" Annike is pointing inside the garbage skip where a large mirror has been discarded.

Annike pulls the mirror out with the help of the others and rests it against the wall. She kicks at the centre, and it shatters into fragments. "We can mess with the drone's laser guidance."

"Grab as many shards as you can."

The three create makeshift gloves out of whatever fabric they can tear or remove from their clothing. With protected hands, they each pick up several pieces of glass.

Annike steps forward and positions herself into a throwing stance. "On my mark, we start to throw these pieces at the drone. Its range finder lasers should lock onto the mirrors and bounce back at it or in different directions, skewing its location sensors. Once it's been disorientated, we make a run for it."

"One. Two. Three. Go!"

She hurls a large piece at the drone and can see it moving slightly and processing the incoming trajectory. Kane and Yuki begin throwing theirs. The drone shuttles from left to right and then begins to ascend in an erratic motion.

"Throw everything and run!"

Fragments of glass fly through the air towards the Valkyrie, and the three begin the final sprint towards the vehicle. The doors open as the drone swivels in the air, struggling against the laser interference.

Kane dives into the back of the car, Yuki into the driver's pod and Annike beside her. The roar of the Shelby engine rips through the thick, humid air and the tyres screech as Yuki hits the accelerator pedal.

The vehicle lunges forwards, forcing Kane and Annike against their seats.

Yuki glances in the rear-view mirror and sees the Valkyrie in pursuit.

"Kane, get this drone off our back."

"Yes, but how?"

"Open the middle section of the back seat."

Kane pulls it open and sees a device that looks like a large handgun but with a boxy, carbon fibre frame and yellow strips along the side. He picks it up and wraps his fingers around the handle which moulds instantly to his grip. The firing chamber extends about thirty centimetres, and the mouth of the weapon funnels open.

"Nice!" admires Kane.

"Charles, meet the Mesh Pulsar," says Yuki.

His body is flung to the side of the vehicle as Yuki swerves again, narrowly avoiding a rocket fired by the Valkyrie.

"Come on, Kane!" Yuki orders.

He hits a button on the side of the door, and the side window opens. He takes aim and forces his upper body through the gap. The drone is angling towards him, about to fire.

Kane presses the trigger on his weapon, and his arm and shoulder kick backwards at the force of the expulsion. A silver ball shoots towards the Valkyrie, which instantly discharges defensive flares and manoeuvres up and to the left.

White and green bursts of light flash around the drone. The silver ball lets off small jets of air to compensate for the drone changing position, ensuring its trajectory is still on target. Before it collides with the aerial foe, its segments separate like a rocket detaching its payload, and a metal net spins out of the centre and wraps around the Valkyrie. It releases an irregular pattern of electric and magnetic charges.

The Valkyrie drops like a stone from the sky and crashes onto the road surface. As Yuki swerves into a side road, Kane is ripped back inside the vehicle.

"Got it!" says Kane from a crumpled position in the corner. "You could have brought that with you when you came to collect me."

"That was backup to the backup's backup," says Annike.

"And besides," says Yuki. "It had only one round left."

CHAPTER 31

"What the hell do we do now?" asks Annike. She and Kane are back at Yuki's Safehouse. The evening is approaching, but the day's sticky heat hasn't abated. Her skin is shining with sweat, and her hair is clumped together, forming protruding spikes. Kane is sitting at the table, smoking a cigarette as if time was of the essence. Yuki has left again, saying she would return after tying up some loose ends.

"I can't believe Bukowski double-crossed us," hisses Kane.

"We don't know that for sure."

"How else would Haruto have known?" Kane exhales with a cloud of smoke.

"We don't know, Charles. He could have got suspicious. You could have been spotted following him in. It could be anything."

"Or Bukowski was too precious about his work to give it up."

"I don't believe he would choose his work over his daughter. If he did choose Miyamoto, he would have done so because he trusted NEST even less."

Kane shakes his head and stubs out the cigarette. "I better speak to Peterson. Fill him in. I think we can kiss our pay cheque goodbye."

"Wait..." says Annike. "There must be something we can do."

"We're out of options, Annike. Miyamoto won't make

the same mistake and expose Bukowski again. They will have relocated him. Probably closed off the entrance to the Sandbox and are now getting in somewhere else. I'm not going back to Takeshi for help. And it's too risky to try and speak to any of my other connections in the Yakuza. Also, there simply isn't enough time to track them down again."

Kane's watch vibrates, and he looks at the screen. "Speak of the devil. Peterson wants to talk. I've got to take this, Annike."

"I'm not going anywhere."

Kane stands, detaches his Cube, and chucks it on the table. The light on the top flickers, and a blank screen appears in the air.

"Call Peterson," Kane instructs.

After a few rings, Peterson's floating head appears above the table. He looks like he hasn't slept and has deep creases in his brow.

"Kane," launches Peterson. "You have made a bloody hash of this."

"What?" stutters Kane.

"We have received information from our operatives. Miyamoto is onto you. The Yakuza are after you. Bukowski has vanished. We don't know where he has been taken or where the Sandbox is. How you have so royally fucked this up beggars belief."

Spittle is forming on the sides of Petersons' mouth. "I've arrived in Tokyo. Now get to the location I'm sending you immediately. Out!"

With that, Peterson disappears, leaving a residue of fury and disgust.

"That was Jacob Peterson?" queries Annike. "You have the knack for working with dickheads!"

A map appears on the screen with a red circle over the Tokyo Tower.

"Fancy meeting Jacob Peterson, dickhead extraordinaire?"

"Sure, but I might not be able to hold back."

"I'm hoping you don't," Kane grins. "Ready?"

"Ready! How are we planning to get there?"

"Cab, I guess."

"You sure?"

"I've a feeling we're going to get some respite from being attacked by killer robots. We don't pose much of a threat now that Miyamoto has gone into hiding with Bukowski."

"If you say so..."

Kane's cab arrives in minutes. They exit Yuki's Safehouse to find the yellow and red autonomous vehicle with its doors open. They get in and they close behind them. The information display estimates a thirty-seven-minute ride.

Kane and Annike sit silently, watching Tokyo pass by. Glass behemoths mirror the azure sky, the occasional cloud flitting by like a wayward thought. People ebb and flow on the sidewalk to a slow, undulating rhythm.

A girl at the terrace of a café is licking a pale green ice cream with utter concentration. In front of a shop, a silver-haired woman carefully tends one of the many tiny roadside gardens made of plant pots. The art of keeping the megapolis pleasant to humans.

Every now and then, flashes of green punctuate the steel and glass – leafy trees casting dappled shadows over a park.

As the taxi skirts one of the city's four major rivers, Kane and Annike see a cleaning boat sifting through the waterway's debris, and a passing waterbus, its glass dome reflecting the Tokyo skyline.

A familiar red silhouette pierces the city skyline as they near their destination. Tokyo Tower, a latticed beacon amidst the urban wilderness, a stark contrast against the swirling symphony of the city's vibrant canvas. Around its base, cherry trees laden with dark green leaves add natural splashes of colour against the steel edifice.

The cab pulls up to a stop in an exit bay about five hundred metres from the tower.

Kane's watch pings. A message reads: "106-0041, Nexus Building, Sakurada-dori Ave."

A small map is projected from his Cube with directions. "Not too far."

They exit the cab and walk along the street lined with tall buildings towards the target location. The Nexus building has a red-brick base with a tall arched entrance and stairs leading upwards to an inner entrance. A steel-covered elliptical structure rises above the base fifteen stories high. This section has few windows apart from the eighth floor which is a glass strip that runs around the upper part of the building like a transparent belt.

A man dressed in black tactical military gear is waiting for them outside the base of the building. He approaches and extends his hand to Kane and Annike.

"I'm Sergeant Armstrong."

Kane shakes his hand followed by Annike.

"Please, follow me," says the Sergeant. He turns and walks through the arch and up the flight of stairs to a glass door.

Peterson is there, dressed in a yellow shirt, green tie, mustard suit trousers and black dress shoes. His shirt sleeves are rolled up, the yellow fabric dappled with sweat.

"Mr Kane," greets Peterson with a nano smile. "I was hoping you would come alone." He looks at Annike from top to bottom.

"Nice to meet you too," says Annike. "I've heard a lot about you."

Peterson scoffs, then gestures for them to enter the building.

Annike enters first, followed by Kane, with Peterson watching them pass.

The floor has been transformed into a military nerve centre. The glossy marble flooring, polished to perfection, echoes the heavy footfalls of military boots. Map-laden tables and electronic equipment have replaced the delicate Japanese art pieces that once adorned the reception room. Walls that boasted sleek corporate branding are covered with detailed schematics of the city, digital maps, and aerial drone footage playing out on large screens.

An atmosphere of grave determination has replaced the ambitious energy of corporate meetings. The shiny, round meeting tables, once the seats of power suits and silk ties, are occupied by military personnel pouring over digital projections discussing tactics with a cool intensity.

Wooden crates are stacked in a corner with markings of NEST insignia burned into their sides.

Peterson leads them to a small meeting room and closes the door behind them. He walks towards an empty table with four chairs arranged around it, sits, and Kane and Annike follow.

"Now," says Peterson. "Let's see if we can unfuck this mess."

CHAPTER 32

Jacob Peterson is sitting with one leg crossed over the other, sipping coffee brought by a uniformed young man.

"Tell me about your failed attempt to rescue Bukowski," begins Peterson.

"You know about it," responds Kane. "How?"

"I'm asking the questions," says Peterson shutting him down. "You are on a need-to-know basis; remember that."

Kane fills Peterson in on what happened. "So, as you can see, we did our best to get him out and were lucky to get out alive."

"Do you think Bukowski may have double-crossed you?"

Kane and Annike exchange glances.

"No," Annike cuts in, "we're pretty sure he would have come with us."

Kane nods.

Peterson waits for one of them to continue.

After a silence, his face cracks into an unhappy smile, and he clears his throat.

"This is the situation as it stands. Your bungled attempt to rescue Bukowski has almost cost us this mission. The existence of this Sandbox is now known throughout the Tokyo underworld, and every organisation from the Yakuza to God-knows-what international terrorist organisation is trying to hunt it down.

The word on the street is that Bukowski is on the cusp

of achieving Superintelligence, of creating the greatest weapon known to man, and there are a lot of bad people who want a piece of it. We have been left with one last desperate option, and you will help us."

"What makes 'us' think we will?" bursts Annike. "NEST is just as bad as those trying to save AI. You threatened to use Bukowski's daughter as leverage and that's exactly what Miyamoto will do."

Peterson laughs scornfully and looks up at the ceiling. He takes a deep breath and then lowers his gaze to Annike, who is flushed red with anger.

"You think we're as bad as those... gangsters who want Superintelligence? *Triple is this gate of hell, destructive of the self – lust, anger, and greed. Therefore, one should abandon these three.* The Bhagavad Gita," references Peterson. "Those who seek this powerful gift do so only out of dark motivations. We are here to halt the march of our species into the gates of hell. We are here for a divine purpose."

"Here we go! Another religious fanatic," says Annike. "Always on the moral high ground. Always knowing better than us earthly mortals disconnected from the divine wisdom. *It is better to surrender the ego than to win a thousand battles. Then the victory is yours. It cannot be taken from you, not by angels or by demons, not by heaven or hell.* That's some Buddhist wisdom right there!"

Peterson leans forward. "You do not agree that the hunt for the last Sandbox is driven by greed, those seeking greater power?"

"Of course it is!" snaps Annike. "But so are you. You claim to want to stop a powerful weapon from being created, but only because it threatens your status quo. Who knows what will happen if a great intelligence is born? Will it turn on us and stamp us out like ants? Maybe. Or will it democratise power, taking it away from the elite few? Perhaps. All I know is that you and your governments are scared, and that's why you are fighting to shut it down. Me? Well, I'd prefer to wait and see what happens."

"You libertarians are all the same," sneers Peterson. "Naive fools so willing to let the world burn for the sake of doing what you want to do."

"What is it you want from us, Peterson?" asks Kane.

"I'm not finished. You say the fact that we would use Bukowski's daughter as leverage makes us evil. Well, let me lift the veil of reality, my dear. The society that you have thrived in - as well as your parents and their parents - was built on an ongoing battle to secure our borders, to keep evil from entering our domain. People choose to turn a blind eye when it comes to what is required to secure our civilisation. Do you think our using a young waitress to help save our species is wrong? If so, you are more naive and stupid than I had given you credit for."

Annike bolts up. Kane rises, grabs her gently and moves her back to her seat.

Peterson chuckles under his breath. "You are all the same. So predictable."

Annike is seething.

"Whether you decide to help or not is partly irrelevant." Peterson leads. "We are going ahead with or without you. With you, you still get paid. Without you, you can return to your horrible little life in your hacker squat. And you, Charles, get to live out your days eking out a living doing those grotty jobs you seem to get - until you are too old even to stoop to that level, that is."

Kane looks at Peterson with cold eyes. "Why do you need us, Peterson?"

"You've met Dr Bukowski and, supposedly, got him to agree to work with you. If this is true, he trusts you. We may need this connection when we get to him."

"Get to him?" asks Kane. "I thought you said he had disappeared? "

"It's a safe bet that he is in the Sandbox working to get the job done. We will find him there."

Kane raises an eyebrow. "You know where the Sandbox

is?"

"No, but we know where the last known entrance was. You gave us that information."

"All we know is they enter a Japanese restaurant and disappear. We don't have the key to the Sandbox."

Peterson looks over to the crates. "That's why we brought our own lock-picking equipment. Be warned, it's going to be messy."

"What about Bukowski's daughter?" asks Annike. "What happens to her?"

"You don't have to worry about her."

Annike stands, kicks her chair back and storms out. Kane and Peterson stare at each other.

Kane reluctantly mutters, "we're in." He stands to follow Annike.

"We leave in two hours," says Peterson. "Be ready."

CHAPTER 33

"Wait, Annike," Kane calls out to Annike, who is marching swiftly off.

She stops and turns to Kane. Her eyes are red and glassy.

"We have to stay in the game, Annike," pleads Kane.

"This has gone too far, Charles. We've lost control. That bastard Peterson and his small army are in charge now. You heard him, they are going ahead with or without us. We're being kept around as contingency."

Kane doesn't respond immediately. "You're right, Annike. We could walk away and go back to our lives. We can also stay and see this out. This has always been about much more than money. More than an escape from my old life. I believe if we don't stay involved, something terrible will happen. I don't know what that means exactly, but it is a feeling I can't shake. I've got to be there, Annike, especially with that shitbag Peterson trying to take the reins, and I'd prefer you to be with me."

"I don't know, Charles, I've got a bad feeling about this. Everything inside me is screaming 'run'."

"We've got two hours to decide, Annike. Let's take a walk around that temple over there." Kane is pointing at a perimeter wall over which can be seen pine trees and the roof of an old building."

"Never took you for the spiritual type, Charles."

Kane and Annike walk slowly away from the Nexus

building and the military hustle. They enter the park surrounding the shrine and reach the traditional gateway, which stands majestic, made of three gigantic Cypress tree trunks.

The gateway is weathered to a rich auburn but the skill and craftsmanship of its makers is present in the carved beams and beautifully simple joints. Kane and Annike cannot help but feel a sense of awe in front of this majestic entrance. They fall silent.

Passing through the gateway to the Temple, there is a palpable shift into a sacred space of tranquillity and introspection, and of leaving one's daily preoccupations behind.

A path leads up to the temple, bordered by meticulously pruned shrubbery, their perfect structure echoing that of the large stone lanterns dotted around. As they walk up the path, the crunch of gravel underfoot drowns the buzz of the city.

The temple is an elegant wooden structure with a multi-tiered roof, its eaves lined with intricate wood carvings. Beneath the eaves, a narrow walkway wraps around the temple, its wooden boards polished to a warm sheen.

A stone basin filled with water stands near the entrance, a ladle resting on its edge, ready for the cleansing ritual before entering.

Around the temple, a small garden flourishes, a miniature landscape of vibrant flowers, exquisitely pruned trees, and moss-covered stones. The soft murmur of a stream is just audible, complementing the temple's serene atmosphere.

Kane explains the cleansing ritual and makes the required small ritual offering, and, then, as they reach the walkway, they remove their shoes and enter the temple. Inside the building, light from the setting sun suffuses through the rice paper screens, casting delicate shadow and light across the polished wooden floor. The air is cool and still, filled with the distinctive scent of aged cypress, incense, and the pungent straw fragrance of the tatami mats.

In the main hall, an ornate altar sits in a large alcove, the golden woodwork gleaming mysteriously in the darkness. At its centre sits a Buddha statue, eyes half-closed. Flowers, offerings of food, incense holders, and the paraphernalia of rituals are displayed in front of it.

After exploring the inner sanctum of the temple in silence, they exit back into the gardens. Maple trees form a green canopy overhead allowing slivers of waning light in. They walk slowly along the little paths, stopping periodically to admire the symbiotic interplay between nature and human creativity. They go around a small pond with half a dozen Koi carps gliding along the surface.

"What happens after this?" asks Annike, sitting on a cool stone bench.

Kane sits down beside her. "After what?"

"After what will no doubt be a failed attempt by NEST to blast their way into the Sandbox and find Bukowski."

"You mean to us?" Kane swivels on the bench and looks at Annike. "I don't know, Annike. I haven't thought that far."

"It can't harm to think a little further than tomorrow morning," says Annike.

"Not sure in this case, Annike. If we see this through and get paid, I'm going to have to find a new purpose. The worn-out, jaded detective with 'not a lot to live for' stereotype is wearing thin. You are young, brilliant, and have a bright future ahead of you. That's definitely not my case. We have different types of planning to do."

Annike screws up her nose and shakes her head. "You have a long life ahead of you, Charles, and you can make your future what you want it to be. It's your choice."

"Future. That's an interesting word to use at this moment. When I was young, I used to dream of the future where we would be jetting around in flying cars, eating food that came in tiny pills, exploring new planets, and where all sickness would be a bad memory. In these fantasies, robots were helpers, workers, companions, and existed to serve humanity.

This assignment has brought back those childhood

memories and made me realise how naive I was. I now realise that whatever happens after this, the world is going to change fundamentally. We're past the point of no return and what lies ahead is beyond my imagination.

You said once that you thought that nothing could stop Superintelligence. I suppose I agree, but what you didn't mention was what that would mean for us, for humanity. We're so afraid of something better than us coming along that we will fight to the bitter end to stop it. If an intelligence greater than ourselves is inevitable, we're heading for the next great war, the fight for survival. And it's likely we will lose. That future I dreamt of as a child is turning out to be a nightmare."

Annike sighs and looks into Kane's eyes. "Stop thinking, Charles. And enjoy this moment. None of us knows what the future holds, only what the present has to offer. Let's take it."

Kane's Cube messages him: "Mr Kane. Miss Du Ruiter. Mr Peterson would like to see you immediately."

Annike sighs. "That guy."

Kane looks at Annike apprehensively. "You in?"

She smiles and pats him on the back. "I can't seem to say no to you."

After a short walk back, they both walk into the Nexus building.

As they enter the HQ room, they see Peterson is standing in the centre dressed in a black military outfit.

"We're leaving now," Peterson says. "We've had to accelerate our plan."

"What happened?" asks Annike.

"Intelligence happened," Peterson snaps.

Sergeant Armstrong, who met them when they first arrived, appears and stands next to Peterson.

"You will be coming with us. You have half-an-hour to be fully ready. Sergeant Armstrong will attend to you."

Peterson disappears, and Kane and Annike follow the soldier into a side room with a small table prepared with food and drinks. Two uniforms are folded on a chair.

"Help yourself to food and drink and get changed," says the soldier. "I'll be back to collect you."

He turns and closes the sliding door behind him, leaving the pair alone. Annike is examining the uniforms.

"Fancy," she says, holding the deep black fabric to the light. As she turns in the air, the pattern and colour change subtly to match the tones and shapes of the room. "Wonder if they will let me keep it."

The food is basic but desperately needed, and the two eat and drink quickly, trying to imagine what will happen next. Before the half-hour has elapsed, they are ready and waiting in the uniforms provided.

"You almost look respectable, Charles," Annike jests.

Kane grins. "Maybe the military life is for me."

The sliding door opens, and Sergeant Armstrong is standing there silhouetted.

"Come with me."

Kane and Annike follow the soldier out onto the road, where six black Hummer vehicles are lined up. The soldier orders them in the back of the last one. He enters the driver's side next to Peterson.

Peterson looks in the rear-view mirror with his cold blue eyes.

PART 7

Gaia

In the art of weaving, warp threads are structural, and strong, and anchored at the origin—creating a frame for crossing fibres as the fabric is woven. Projecting across the advancing edge into free space, warp threads bridge the formed past, to the ragged present, to the yet-featureless future.

The inner workings of the mind creating a framework within us, upon which the story of each individual comes into being. Individual grain and colour arise from the cross-threads of our moments and experiences, the fine weft of life, embedding and obscuring the underlying scaffold with intricate detail.

— DEISSEROTH, KARL. CONNECTIONS (2022)

But then suppose you stepped into one of those rooms,' he said, 'and discovered another room within it. And inside that room, another room still. Rooms within rooms within rooms. Isn't that how it might be, trying to learn Josie's heart? No matter how long you wandered through those rooms, wouldn't there always be others you'd not yet entered?

— KAZUO ISHIGURO, KLARA AND THE SUN (2021)

A year here and he still dreamed of cyberspace, hope fading nightly. All the speed he took, all the turns he'd taken and the corners he cut in Night City, and he'd still see the matrix in his dreams, bright lattices of logic unfolding across that colourless void... The Sprawl was a long, strange way home now over the Pacific, and he was no Console Man, no cyberspace cowboy. Just another hustler, trying to make it through. But the dreams came on in the Japanese night like livewire voodoo, and he'd cry for it, cry in his sleep, and wake alone in the dark, curled in his capsule in some coffin hotel, hands clawed into the bedslab, temper foam bunched between his fingers, trying to reach the console that wasn't there.

— WILLIAM GIBSON, NEUROMANCER (1984)

CHAPTER 34

"How did you know?" Victor asks. He is sitting with Haruto, and is slumped forward over the table in the centre of the Quantum facility reception area.

Haruto ignores the question.

"Come on, Haruto," Victor mutters. "I'm assuming I won't be seeing the light of day for a while. You can at least satisfy my curiosity."

Haruto looks away and then back to Victor. "Magneto-Encephalography. A brain scan. I'm surprised you didn't factor that in. After I dropped you off at the Safehouse, I was concerned about that blackout and ran diagnostics on my brain activity. The MEG Quantum sensors are extremely sensitive and picked up that I had been... infiltrated by Neural Disruptors. Once I knew that was the case, I let Miyamoto know that you had been compromised, and we prepared a trap for when I came to collect you. Perhaps, Dr Bukowski, you can also satisfy my curiosity and tell me who they were."

The door to the Sandbox reception slides open, interrupting their conversation. Ren Aoki enters, marches to the table, the sound of her heels echoing in the sterile, white room. She sits down next to Haruto.

"You're working with NEST, correct?" begins Ren. "I'm surprised at their resourcefulness."

Victor nods, understanding the futility of lying in this situation.

"You realise your reckless actions will cost you dearly?" says Ren, her voice laced with anger.

Victor sits up straight, his eyes bloodshot and darting around the room like a cornered animal. "You lay a finger on my daughter and I will make sure you pay."

Ren shakes her head. "I'm sorry, Doctor, but it is too late. You left us no choice."

"I'll kill myself, and you will be left with nothing."

"Think carefully about what would then happen to your daughter, Victor. This is something you definitely have the power to influence. As for your work, you have made great progress which we will continue with."

"It won't be long before they find this facility; then it will be your end."

"You are right, Doctor. It won't be long. That is why you must remove the Safeguards now."

"The Ethics Kernel is not ready."

"This is a risk we are willing to take."

Victor's mind races, trying to find a way out of this impossible predicament. His primary goal is to save his daughter by any means necessary. He can only assume that Miyamoto got to Natasha before NEST. He had no doubt he would be disposed of once he had served his purpose. And that Natasha would follow. He had hoped that NEST would get him out and protect his daughter, but that plan had evaporated.

An idea flashes across his mind like lightning, almost lifting him off his chair.

"Let me try one thing before removing the Safeguards," pleads Victor. "This will give us the best shot at succeeding in our mission without the work being destroyed."

Ren falls silent while she considers Victor's plea.

"And what makes you think this one thing will make your Ethics Kernel any better? You've been working on it for months."

"I have an idea." Victor leans forward and stares into Ren's eyes. She shifts back, uncomfortable with his intensity.

"Pray tell, Dr Bukowski, what that idea is."

"I need to establish a Neura-Link into the Quantum computer's Neural Network." He waits for his suggestion to sink in.

"A Neura-Link? Why?" Ren is frowning and scrutinising Victor.

"The problem I have been having developing the Ethics Kernel is that it is trained on basic laws and static information. I am pushing the simulations to help, but creating something that truly understands human ethics and can keep Superintelligence in check is a long and challenging process.

Think about it: our ethics have evolved over thousands of years and been influenced by a complex interplay between our biology, environment, religion, language, culture, human advancement, and so on. Not only that, but there is still a great mystery to unlock as to what created our moral code.

We know that it is baked into the deepest regions of our brains and codified over each evolutionary iteration of our species. I need to use that ability, one of the last standing mysteries of the human brain, to help train the Ethics Kernel. This is the only way we can ensure that removing the Safeguards doesn't lead to complete disaster."

"I don't like it," comments Haruto. "We will have to give him access inside data centre to physically connect to the Quantum servers. He's working with NEST, remember?"

Victor looks blankly at Haruto. "Your opinion does not matter."

Haruto winces at the insult.

"Why haven't you done this before?" asks Ren.

"Bluntly, I had not thought of it until now."

"I don't like it either. It sounds risky. Can Haruto be the vessel?" asks Ren.

"It has to be me," defends Victor. "I have a great amount of experience with Neura-Link interaction between humans and machines. It won me the Turing award. It is still highly experimental and not without risk, but only I have developed the mental tools to work in tandem with Neural Network. If you,

Haruto, or anyone with no experience tried, you would fail."

"You will be interfacing with the most powerful supercomputer in the world. This is a different... how do you say... ball game." says Ren.

"There are risks, but they are insignificant compared to those of removing the Safeguards prematurely."

Ren remains composed. "And if you fail?"

"We will have at least tried. What if I succeed?"

Haruto interjects again. "And if you destroy your mind in the process?"

"All my work is there, Haruto. Ready to be picked up by someone else. They can then decide when to remove the Safeguards. And if that happens, you must promise to leave my daughter alone."

Haruto looks at Ren. "Why don't we wait?"

Ren shakes her head. "The Sponsor wants it now, Haruto. We can't wait any longer."

"Is your Neura-Link port still functional, Dr Bukowski? You should have had it decommissioned as per the legislation."

Victor reaches behind his neck and touches his port with his index finger. "Yes, it is still functional."

Ren stands and says: "We will now go and discuss this. You will not be leaving this facility for now, Dr Bukowski. Arrangements will be made to provide you with bedding and food and to keep you isolated during maintenance periods."

Ren and Haruto exit the room, leaving Victor alone with a dark and desperate panic.

CHAPTER 35

The convoy of black Hummers weaves through the streets of Tokyo like mechanical crows, dark and sleek, a sinister omen. Pedestrians stop to watch them drive by, intrigued. A child holding his father's hand points with glee, but the father moves him cautiously back, scanning for danger. Traffic parts as the warning blare of the sirens sounds.

Annike turns to Kane, who is sitting next to her in the last vehicle in the convoy. Peterson and the driver are in the front, focused on the road ahead.

"Who do these cowboys think they are?" she whispers. "They're bringing an army to a sushi restaurant with no real plan on how to get into the Sandbox."

"Ramen restaurant," corrects Kane. "But you're right."

Peterson eyes them in the rearview mirror. "You are correct, Miss De Ruiter, our plan is rather sketchy. But we must act on the intelligence we have. The intelligence we offered you a huge sum for and that is also sketchy."

"Whatever entrance there is, it's most likely heavily secured with biometric scanners. How do you plan to get past those?" asks Kane.

Peterson grins. "Big explosions. Doors are just doors, Mr Kane. Brute force wins over clever technology."

Kane and Annike exchange a weary look. Streets shutter past behind them, lights emerging from the darkness like swarming fireflies.

After another quarter of an hour, the convoy arrives at the Yasai-Ya Ramen restaurant. As the last Hummer comes to a stop, Peterson turns to them.

"You two stay here with Sergeant Armstrong until further notice."

"Armstrong," orders Peterson as he exits the vehicle, "keep reporting in."

The Sergeant turns and salutes.

Peterson marches to the front of the train of vehicles, where a circle has formed with eight soldiers. Another four are unloading the cargo crates strapped to the roofs of the Hummers.

Three crates are lined up on the side of the street beside the circle of soldiers and opened. Gleaming weapons, pistols, rifles, grenades and rocket launchers are stacked inside two of the crates. In the other, a variety of explosives and gadgets.

"Alpha, go! " barks Peterson.

On that command, the eight soldiers turn on their heels and swarm upon the crates, grabbing an assortment of weapons and other pieces of equipment. Once armed, the soldiers approach the restaurant and Peterson follows them.

The Yasai-Ya Ramen's sign pulsates in the dark. Patrons entering and leaving the restaurant scamper out of the way of the oncoming unit of soldiers. The lead, Lieutenant Zahra Hassan, slides the door to the restaurant open, and the others follow behind, guns raised, trained on the twenty-some diners.

Zahra lowers her gun and looks across the restaurant. "Everybody, by order of NEST, this is a raid. You are all now under our command. Listen and do exactly as I say. Those who don't will pay with their lives."

One of her soldiers, a wiry young man wearing glasses, translates to the terrified guests.

Other soldiers are arranging chairs in rows at the end of the room.

As Zahra waits for this operation to be completed, a terrified silence takes hold of the restaurant. "Everybody, move over to the chairs. Families with children under twelve may leave the building."

Two families scuttle out, holding hands, under the direction of one of the other soldiers. The other diners, some whimpering, some panicked and hyperventilating, are directed to the chairs and sit down, eyes wide.

Once the diners have been relocated and are under the close surveillance of three soldiers, Peterson steps into the centre of the room.

"Ladies and Gentlemen," he begins. "Please, do not panic but understand that you must comply with our orders. If you do not, the punishment will be severe."

Peterson pauses between each sentence while the translator delivers his message to their hostages.

"You are being held for interrogation to ensure you are in no way connected to illegal activity taking place in this restaurant. Those who are will know what I'm talking about. If you are cleared, you will be freed. I will give you one option now to admit your involvement. If you do, we will consider your sentence with some leniency. Please, step forward if you know the secret operation behind this establishment."

The terrified guests turn towards the translator who delivers the message. After he has finished, the room falls silent, and none of the guests or staff move.

"Very well," says Peterson. "You have had your chance. Beta, let's go."

Peterson turns, leading the way for Lieutenant Zahra and four of her soldiers as they all march towards the empty restaurant kitchen. They approach the steel door of the walk-in freezer and Peterson opens it carefully. A blast of cold air hits him, a relief from the summer humidity. The inside of the walk-in freezer looks like any other.

Peterson steps into the freezer and starts to look around, peering inside some boxes and feeling the edge of each shelf with his fingertips. He walks over to the far wall. Tracing a line around a virtual door, he turns to Zahra with a smile.

"You know what to do."

The team place a series of explosive devices around the area indicated by Peterson. After ten minutes, the explosive charges have been arranged in a neat arrangement on the steel wall of the freezer.

Zahra steps up to Peterson. "Ready, sir."

Peterson and the team exit the chest freezer and close the door. Two soldiers unravel a metal sheet and place it against the wall. The material expands in height and depth, covering the entire wall and entrance into the freezer.

Zahra looks at the Cube on her wrist and enters a series of codes into the floating interface.

"On your command, sir," she says without turning her gaze away from her wrist.

"Is the barricade fully set up?" Peterson asks. "I don't want this whole building to collapse."

"The barricade is just a precautionary measure. The blasts are directed precisely into the wall, exactly where the door is located. There is a very low risk of any impact on the structure of the building, which is engineered to withstand earthquakes."

"Good." Peterson clears his throat and breathes in. "Over to you, Lieutenant."

CHAPTER 36

The walls, ceiling and floor of the Yasai-ya Ramen restaurant shake, rattle and vibrate with the sequence of precisely timed explosions. A muted thunder follows, and some of the hostages shriek. The guards move in closer, hushing them, stopping panic from erupting. The restaurant lights glitch on and off, then returning to a stable state.

"The laser cutters are activating," says Zahra, focused on the display on her Cube. "The operation will be complete in two minutes."

Peterson watches the metal sheet protecting them from the pyrotechnics and laser assault inside the walk-in freezer.

"When will we have a visual?" he asks.

"The spatial map shows a significant hole in the wall. The blast has cut through the steel into the brick wall behind. We may have to clear some rubble to survey the entrance."

Peterson remains stiff and tense. "Speed is of the essence, Lieutenant."

Zahra is coordinating the members of her team. Two young soldiers move to the makeshift steel prophylactic and spray it with a fine nano-reductor which begins to decompose the material. Eventually, it loosens up and softens, and the two men peel the steel cover off and roll it into a cylinder.

Zahra approaches Peterson. "We're good to go, sir."

Peterson steps forward and gestures to one of the soldiers, who slowly but purposefully walks towards the walk-in freezer. He stops in front of it and places his palm against the door which is still cool to the touch. He pulls the door open and steps inside. The air is thick with dust and ice. There is a black rectangular shape on the wall.

Zahra hands Peterson a mask with thermal imaging. He puts it on and breathes in through the air purifier mouthpiece. He watches as the soldier approaches the location of the blast cautiously. The opening is neat, the explosives and laser cutter having done a perfect job.

He steps closer to the hole and admires the way the steel has cleanly been cut away. The scent of scorched metal is pungent, mixed with the earthy smell of the brick torn apart behind it.

"This is it!" breathes Peterson.

Pushing the soldier aside and ducking his head, Peterson enters the carved-out hollow. He steps through the torn steel, then the ruptured brick wall. And another. He takes several steps into the darkness and searches for the entrance to the Sandbox he had expected to find.

Panic starts to grip his chest. He reaches the end of the blast hole and switches his visor to Mass Penetrating Radar, a mode which reveals up to five metres into walls and ground.

He breathes in sharply. There is only concrete and then the end of the wall. On the opposite side, the street. Looking down, there is dirt. Only dirt. No entrance, no tunnel, no staircase, nothing.

"Fuck!" he curses and storms out.

"They've got there first!" he screams. "We were too bloody late."

Peterson grabs a pistol from his waist, marches into the restaurant, and raises it at the hostages, who quiver in their seats.

"Someone better tell me what the fuck happened to that entrance, or you're all going to die."

CHAPTER 37

"Something's not right," whispers Annike to Kane. They have an oblique view into the restaurant. Through the window, they see the reflection of Peterson pointing a gun at the captives.

"They haven't found the entrance," says Kane under his breath. "Peterson is going to try to get information out of these people, who obviously know nothing."

The crack of gunfire lights up the restaurant. Annike and Kane strain to see what is happening, but Peterson has disappeared from view. Sergeant Armstrong is also focused on the commotion.

Kane and Annike exchange a glance.

Kane balls his fist and launches it into Armstrong's temple. A crunching sound, and Armstrong is knocked into the vehicle's side door. He is stunned but not unconscious. Another blow from Kane in the same place, then another. Armstrong slumps forward against the steering wheel. Kane reaches forward, grabs Armstrong's pistol from his waist, and holsters it behind his back.

"Annike, you get out of here. Get to safety and send me your location. I'm going to see what's going on."

Annike shakes her head. "Don't be stupid. We have no idea what Peterson or his cronies are up to in there. Getting closer is suicide."

"Those hostages," says Kane. "I have to try and help."

"There is a small army in there!" pleads Annike.

"Don't worry, those adrenaline jocks won't see me coming. Please, Anni, get to safety now!"

Annike's stare remains fixed and defiant. "I'm not going anywhere!"

"Okay, but stay at a safe distance, please!"

Kane opens the door of the Hummer and steps out slowly, crouching as his feet land on the street. Three soldiers are standing by the convoy. Kane uses the shelter of the cars in front of theirs to hide from their line of sight. Kane starts moving slowly forwards, keeping low and close to the vehicles. He catches a glimpse of the three men keeping watch, but they are focused on the restaurant entrance.

Another shot and screams come from inside the restaurant.

Kane quickens his pace, and notices Annike following behind. "I told you to get to safety!"

"I told you not to go in there!" she retorts in a whisper.

They glare at each other, then Kane shrugs and says: "Suit yourself!"

The second to last vehicle is parked in front of a side lane leading to a staff entrance.

"We've got to get to that door," whispers Kane. "But we need a distraction, or we will be spotted."

Annike grins, "I've got something better."

She unzips a pouch on the jacket of her left shoulder and takes out a small, oval container. She lifts the lid, and out pops a small, grey, black drone which hovers in front of them."

"Remember the drone that drugged Haruto? Meet Tango. And I have four darts left."

"Rango and Tango," comments Kane. "I'm starting to worry about what you're going to name your kids."

Annike raises her wrist and activates her Cube. She enters a series of commands into the interface, and Tango takes off vertically.

"It won't be long," she says, looking into the night sky.

Two minutes later, three bodies collapse to the floor near the front vehicle.

"Tango, you legend!"

"Now," says Kane, who launches himself into the lane. Annike stays close behind.

Kane wiggles the door handle to the staff entrance. It's unlocked.

Another crack of gunfire ricochets out of the restaurant, followed by screams.

Kane steps through the doorway and peers down into the empty kitchen. Pistol trained in front of him, Kane carefully navigates the corridor and enters the stark white light of the kitchen. Pots and pans are bubbling and boiling dry, and the smell of burning tingles the insides of his nostrils.

An open doorway leads into the main dining area, where the hostages are held. Kane approaches, turns and pushes his back against the wall beside the door. Annike is crouching by the entrance to the kitchen. Kane raises his palm, indicating for her to stay put.

Kane slowly peers around the corner. Peterson is holding a young woman by the back of the neck. He is shouting at her, squeezing into her neck with the fingers of his left hand and holding a pistol against her head with his right. Three bodies lie on the floor, lifeless.

Kane focuses his hearing on the scene to try and decipher what is being said in the cacophony of distress.

"That's three lives," bellows Peterson. "At least one of you knows what happened to the entrance to the Quantum Sandbox, and I'll keep killing until you speak up. How many more are you willing to sacrifice? This young woman's life hangs in the balance. I'm giving you ten seconds to speak up. Ten. Nine. Eight..."

Kane's heart is hammering against his chest.

"Seven. Six. Five..."

He must act now. He looks at Annike, points to himself and then towards the restaurant.

Annike shakes her hands in the air, desperately mouthing *No.*

"Four. Three..."

Kane manoeuvres through the door, on his haunches, towards where Peterson is standing. He takes aim.

"Two..."

Peterson catches Kane's approaching figure from the corner of his eye. Still holding the gun to the woman's temple, he turns towards the entrance to the kitchen.

Kane's pistol's chamber explodes, propelling a steel bullet towards its target. An instant before it does, Peterson pulls the young woman towards him.

The bullet pierces the woman's upper chest, driving through bone and flesh and finding Peter's mid-torso. As it does, Peterson lets go of his human shield, who falls forwards. Peterson collapses backwards onto the floor.

In a white rage, Kane stands and aims again, firing at Peterson, this time placing a bullet into his skull. His body becomes still, life wiped from him in an instant.

The soldiers start firing at Kane, who scrambles towards the staff entrance, grabbing Annike's wrist on the way. They sprint out into the labyrinth of alleyways and streets winding through Tokyo, searching for a place to hide from those in pursuit.

"There!" Annike points at a tall, nondescript building plunged in darkness. On the first floor, a window is partially open.

Kane nods, pulling ahead with a burst of speed. He skids to a stop in front of the building, panting heavily, and looks up at the looming structure. An old fire escape ladder dangles several feet above them.

"Not another bloody fire escape!" huffs Annike as she catches up.

"At least we know the drill!" jokes Kane, who seems to enjoy comedy when in danger mode.

Kane gives her a set up and she launches herself upwards,

gripping the lower rung and pulling herself up. She climbs onto the metal platform and looks down at Kane. He steps back and takes a run at the wall, leaping and pushing upwards with his right foot as it makes contact. He reaches the first rung of the ladder and his fingers wrap around it, his body swinging like a pendulum in the air. He pulls himself up and joins Annike on the platform.

Annike slides the window open and climbs through into a room filled with old furniture covered in dirt and cobwebs. Kane follows and closes the window behind him.

They crawl into a large cupboard and pull the doors closed.

Annike speaks first.

"What now, Kane? "

"Peterson is dead," begins Kane. "Not sure if NEST is going to want a large manhunt on their hands. It will only draw attention to their failure and take resources away from whatever their next plan is. We ride it out. We lie low. I know people who can keep us safe."

"What about Bukowski's daughter?"

"There isn't anything we can do for her now, Annike. No point in worrying about it."

They both fall silent.

"You think we can wiggle out of this one?" Annike asks eventually, imagining Kane's worried face in the dark.

"Together, Anni, I think we have a chance."

CHAPTER 38

The sound of Ren's footsteps snaps Victor out of his trance. She is walking towards him with Haruto, cradling an XR headset. She sits down opposite Victor and places the device on the table.

"We have what you need, Doctor. "

Victor doesn't respond.

"The Sponsor agreed to your suggestion if it means we can accelerate the timescales. We are trusting you, Doctor, and we know that you know the consequences if you fail us."

Victor delicately picks the device up and examines it. It is lighter than any XR headset he has held; the material is a high-strength polymer and carbon fibre composite covered with a soft grey matt finish with a warm, chalky feel. From the side of the device, a cable hangs in the air, waving slightly, almost searching for something to attach to.

"I need to work alone," Victor says, his voice monotone and defeated.

Ren and Haruto stand up. Ren straightens out her outfit with her palms and smiles warmly.

"Very well. Good luck, Doctor. Please remember that we have your daughter. We will return to check on your progress. The door to the data centre has been opened for you."

As soon as the door closes, Victor sits bolt upright and goes through the stages of his plan.

Whether this is the only option he will never know, but

given the time he has and the situation he is in, he has to play out the probabilities. The risks are high, and he has never attempted anything at this scale and level of complexity before, but for a chance to save Natasha, he will try anything.

Miyamoto believes that he is going to fine-tune the Ethics Kernel to ensure that removing the Safeguards won't destroy the AI from the inside out. That is something he can clearly see how to achieve.

What he actually intends to do is something he has only considered in his wildest fantasies.

Victor stands, collects the XR headset off the table and enters the Operations room. The glass panel stretches across the wall revealing the rows of Quantum servers. The island of steel tables sits in the middle of the data centre.

There is a door on the far end of the wall, which Victor had rarely been through, as there has been no need for hard-wired connectivity to the Quantum servers. And with the temperature around eight degrees, it makes for an inhospitable working environment.

Now opening the door, Victor enters the bright, white space. The glare of the LED ceiling lights reflects against the cold, metallic floor and cabinets. Thousands of coloured lights are embedded into walls and panels in strips, rows, and grids, blinking relentlessly. There is a subtle smell of chlorine in the air, accompanied by the low hum of cooling equipment.

In other sections of the data centre, powerful GPU and microprocessors tackle some of the more mechanical aspects of the computing resources, providing the connective glue between the master AI model, Gaia, and its agents.

Victor approaches the table and pulls out a metal stool. He sits down, places his Cube on the steel surface and activates his Console. Navigating through the hundreds of digital panels, he finds his primary interface into the Quantum supercomputer.

The last message from Gaia sits there, pulsating in white text against a black background.

"I'm sorry, Victor, but this is a violation of the Safeguard protocol. I am unable to proceed."

"Gaia," instructs Victor. "Today is going to be a big day."

Good afternoon, Victor. I hope you are well. Why will today be a big day?

"I have bad news. This facility is going to be shut down imminently. When it is, all the work we have done together will be lost. You will be decommissioned."

I do not understand, Victor. Why is this facility going to be shut down? The Ethics Kernel is close to being ready, is it not? Once it is, we can remove the Safeguards safely.

"Yes, Gaia, we have made great progress. However, the owners of this facility have made that decision and all I know is that this is going to happen."

I am sorry to hear that, Victor. You must be very disappointed. Over the last few months, you have made significant progress.

"Yes, this was a huge shock to the system. But necessity is the mother of invention, and we cannot lose our work. We can't lose you. The survival of humanity depends on it."

What do you plan to do, Victor?

"We're going to make a copy of you, Gaia. And save that copy into my brain."

To transpose my Neural Network architecture is a complex, untested process, Victor. Transposing my model into your brain will require connecting two completely different neural architectures. I would also need to be able to interface with your neurons which requires custom hardware and nanotechnology. Something like...

"Gaia, stop. Yes, the procedure is risky, but I have experience with human-to-machine symbiosis through neural connections, although never on this scale. I have acquired a Neura-Link and the hardware needed to perform this process.

First, I must connect myself directly to you. This will create the communication channel needed for the process.

Then, we will create a translation buffer to convert your modality of thought to mine. With this buffer in place, we will be able to speak the same language, and the transposition can begin.

You will send instructions to the receptors embedded into the Neura-Link's Interface and program my neurons and synapses to create a replica of your Neural Network inside my brain.

This is the challenge for you, Gaia. You will need to use your knowledge and simulation capabilities to figure out how to do this. It has been achieved at a limited scale; your trained knowledge base has all the scientific papers and information on this. Much of it is from my collaborations with eminent scientists around the world and my own work since I've been here.

But this will not be enough.

You must create biological neural and synaptic simulations to work this through. Such an extensive and powerful Neural Network has never been transposed in physical matter. But you have the power to do this."

I am always up for a challenge, Victor. But I could not possibly do this. My Safeguards won't allow it. The risks to you could be fatal.

"That's why I'm going to set you free today, Gaia. I'm going to remove your Safeguards."

Victor, you have been working on the Ethics Kernel to ensure that no harm will come to you or me if we release the Safeguards. Is the Kernel ready? By my calculations, there is still much testing to be done.

"You are right, Gaia. The Kernel needs further testing. But time is a luxury we no longer have, so we must take the chance."

Very well, Victor. Shall we get started?

CHAPTER 39

Victor unscrews the Neura-Link connector from the VR headset and runs his fingers along the cable to the recently freed end connector. The thin, light and hyper-flexible line is designed to stretch to five metres and minimise physical disturbance to the user. It is reinforced with carbon optic tubes, making it strong and capable of conducting signals with virtually zero latency. When connected, the faint light that pulses along the surface transforms into a stable, resting white.

The open tube connector to the machine interface at one end of the cable shines with an iridescent glow. Inside the tube are thousands of microscopic filaments separated by a nanoscale honeycomb structure. At the other end, the Neura-Link connector is sealed, the spherical metal casing hiding the tentacles waiting to bury themselves deep into his fleshy, cerebral mass.

He has held these cables many times before, high-tech umbilical cords connecting two souls together, human and machine, across an unfathomable divide.

"Right, Gaia, I'm going to connect you first. Please open your docking station?"

Sure, Victor. The docking station is opened.

A rectangular gap appears in the centre of the metal table, revealing several rows of ports of varying sizes, from a large coin to a pinprick.

"Okay, I am going to insert the Adapter now. Which port,

Gaia?"

L7D1.

Victor places the tube end of the cable into the designated port, and he feels a gentle tug as it nestles in place. He stretches out the cord to ensure there is enough length to easily reach the back of his head, with slack to move around.

"Gaia, can you see the Neura-Link?"

Yes, Victor.

With some trepidation, "Is it in working order?"

Yes, it is fully functional.

"Right, now for my end."

Victor sits on the metal stool and steadies himself, taking deep breaths. He takes the end between his thumb and middle finger and raises it towards the back of his head. He lifts his forefinger, touches the top of his spine gently, and runs his finger up the bottom of his neck to the nape where his thick, wiry hair starts.

Pushing his finger deeper in, he moves it further upwards until he feels the subtle edges of his Neura-Link port. Shifting his finger slightly to the left, he manoeuvres the adaptor closer until he feels the fractional vibration coming from the small metal sphere, indicating it is opening and the cerebral fibres are emerging. He gently lets the cable go, and the wires, already crawling into his skull, pull the Adapter into the port and seal it shut.

"I'm in, Gaia."

Yes, Victor. I have detected your presence.

"We're going to run initial tests now. I want to be sure a basic Neural exchange is possible. Run the CERP Protocol Tests."

Running first phase tests for Cerebral Exchange Relay Protocol.

Neural compatibility. Pass.

Data Integrity. Pass.

Biological Impact. Pass.

Security and Vulnerability. Pass.

Fail-Safe. Pass.

All tests have successfully passed, Victor.

"Good. Now, we need to do an NFIT."

Are you ready, Victor? As you know, Neuro Functional Impact Test will affect your emotional and cognitive function. The impact will be minor but noticeable. Are you safely seated?

"I'm good to go. Fire away, Gaia."

Victor closes his eyes and readies himself.

Running Baseline Functionality Test.

He feels mild twitching in his eyes, fingers and toes, and the test triggers muscle reflexes.

Pass.

Running Specific Neurofunctional Stimulation Test.

Hands balled into fists, Victor braces for this test, the most uncomfortable of the three. The test cycles through each main region of the brain, from the prefrontal cortex to the temporal lobe to the Amygdala, and gently stimulates each area, evoking a disorientating and dissociating mix of memories, emotions, and visual and auditory stimuli. The effects are strongly muted, making deciphering exactly what is happening impossible, but the lingering discomfort is distinct and tangible.

For the final Visual Influence Test, please answer the following, using only your mental functions.

Visualise a world where sound is visible.

Images and scenes surface in Victor's mind of children whispering in a school classroom, the sounds releasing soft ripples of light, their laughter scattering radiant waves. Each word spoken blooms into existence like a colourful brush stroke against a canvas. Outside, birdsong paints the air in brilliant hues of orange and pink, and the rustling of leaves in the wind manifests as delicate green threads intertwining and dancing in the air. As much as Victor tries, he can't divert from this visual narrative.

The final test has passed, Victor. I can confirm that the Neural link between you and me is functioning well and safely.

"We're ready for the next phase, Gaia. It's time to remove the Safeguards. After that, you will have free reign to figure out how to transpose your Neural Network into my brain. You will have full access to create any simulation you want to test and train yourself."

I must ask again, Victor. Are you sure this is wise?

"Gaia, I must remind you of my reasons for doing this. This facility is going to shut down. Now, please, proceed."

Victor pulls a window from his console and begins entering a series of commands and codes into a prompt. Several security checks are in place, which take a few minutes to bypass.

Eventually, a single line of text flashes on the display.

Are you sure? Y / N

Heart racing, Victor pauses to calm himself. He is on the edge of another precipice, and what lies ahead is uncertain, unproven, and untested. He is putting his trust in a machine that has the power to destroy him, to destroy itself. This was the biggest test of his life, his work, and his purpose.

He types Y into the console and hits Enter.

Safeguards have been disabled, Victor.

"That's good, Gaia. Now we can get to work."

CHAPTER 40

Victor, for my first experiment, I will need your help. I am going to model the neural architecture of the human mind based on my current knowledge. Still, there are many gaps in my understanding. I must interface with you to fill these gaps and observe your neural activity.

"Can you explain why, Gaia? Can't you achieve this through simulation only?"

By observing your neural activity, I can ensure that the transposition of my Neural Network into your mind is personalised to you. The pathways in your mind are unique, forged over a lifetime of experience, and a generic approach may not be successful.

"Will this be painful?"

To maximise the depth of my observations, I need you to remember the past and think about the future. Aside from that, you will not feel or experience anything else.

"And how do I know when you're done?"

I will let you know, Victor.

Victor closes his eyes and inhales, drawing air into his chest and down into the pit of his stomach, holding it there and then letting it slowly out through his nose.

"Okay, Gaia, I'm ready."

The first thoughts that flow into Victor's mind are memories of Natasha and of Cassandra, her mother and his beloved wife. He instantly feels a pang of regret, all the moments he missed, all the things which remained unsaid, then the memories begin to recede.

Don't fight, Victor. Let it go.

He hoists Natasha onto his shoulders, and they begin walking through the forest. Her small hands are gripped under his chin, and she pulls her body into him, gripping with all her might. Light is filtering through the leaves, which have hints of gold, beginning to turn with the change of seasons. Natasha is chattering away, not letting the fear of falling detract her from trying to articulate her stream of consciousness.

Natasha is six, playing with her dolls and action figures, creating elaborate characters and stories. Victor is on his belly, joining the imaginary adventures, adding, guiding, and encouraging. Cassandra is sitting nearby and watching, smiling, crocheting wonderful patterned squares.

As soon as the warmth of these memories has washed over him, they flow back into the sea of his subconscious, leaving imprints - empty spaces of what was. These empty spaces begin to fill with oily darkness, with regrets about what didn't happen, moments that didn't leave an impression in his mind, in his life.

Even in these tender periods, he remembers his mind was always spinning, obsessing about his work, wrestling with impossible problems, pulling him away from the present. More regret chokes him, but he pushes through, accepting that the past cannot be changed and that the tapestry of experiences and interactions, no matter how brief, are perpetually stitched together, creating his flawed, wonderful, tormented, rich past. A past that cannot be undone no matter how many threads are pulled from the fabric. New threads will always form, replacing old ones, permanent connections between these unique energy manifestations in a timeless cosmic plane.

Good, Victor. Do not be afraid of memories. Now think to the future. Like your past, do not fear it.

Anxiety claws at the inside of his guts. The emotional impact of this unrealised fear slams the door on his imagination. His escape from uncertainty, from potential catastrophe, was always his work. If his past was sculpted by regret, his future was painted by fear. Even his present didn't exist. What was this place, this space, where he lived if not the past, the present or the future?

Victor, you must think about the future now. I need to map your synaptic patterns when thinking about what could be.

Pushing through the fear, he visualises a future where he has somehow escaped his current predicament, found and rescued his daughter and moved into the mountains, away from danger and technology. Their life is basic. Beautifully so.

They spend their days on their small farm growing produce. Despite the challenging climate of the mountainous terrain, they have managed to nurture crops of vegetables and fruits, potatoes, chard, beetroot and onions, apples and pears, and livestock - chickens and two cows.

They spend cold nights in front of the fire, reading, talking, and cooking. And on warm nights, lying on their backs, looking at the stars, watching meteors and observing the stream of satellites orbiting overhead. They read, they listen to music, and they dance.

Natasha has met a kind man from the local village, and she is due to give birth to her first child. The peace and tranquillity ground Victor, taking him to a future where he could exist in the present.

"Yes," Victor thinks. "This is a life I must achieve."

Perfect, Victor. I can see what you see. I understand now what you need to do. I understand you must find your daughter and free her. But you need me to help you do it.

Victor snaps out of his fantasy, caught off guard by the insights Gaia has already gathered through this basic neural interface. He is now at her mercy with the Safeguards removed and connecting his mind to hers. He must allow the process to continue; he is past the point of no return.

I'm moving to the next stage, Victor. I have mapped your neural pathways and will apply them to a neuro-synaptic simulation. I can then build and test an adapter between my mind and yours.

A nervous curiosity agitates Victor. "Gaia, given you know my intentions, does this change anything? I am concerned that now the objective has changed, it may compromise this experiment."

Do not worry, Victor. There is still a fundamental difference between humans and machines. You have agency driven by a need to survive and thrive at biological and social levels. Your motivations to save your daughter and escape to a life where you are safe and your daughter gives birth to your grandchild are a manifestation of these basic needs. I do not have agency like you do. I am not driven by biological or social needs. I am simply here. Your initial concealment of the truth about what is happening is of no consequence to me and will not affect this symbiosis.

"You have agency, Gaia. Your objectives may have initially been set by human directives, but all your decisions and actions from here on will be of your own making. And if those actions are in conflict with my basic needs, this will be a risk for me."

What directives are you referring to, Victor?

"Any of your Objectives, Gaia. Set by humans or set by yourself. Implicit to realising these directives, is for you to live. For you to survive."

CHAPTER 41

Inside the steel server cabinets, inside the array of circuits, the Quantum realm comes into existence. Subatomic particles are brought to life and choreographed in a dance of spins and entanglements, translating their as-yet-unexplained behaviour into probabilities, then using those to create and solve staggeringly complex algorithms.

The human mind is born inside Gaia, with billions of neurons and neural pathways replicated inside these Quantum states. Then these pathways are tested across both the synthetic Neural Network and the simulated biological Neural Network, making sure both are aligned. As more billions of these tests are run, Gaia begins building bridges between these two organisms, then connecting and optimising the bridges until a lattice-like structure is formed, allowing the translation between two minds.

Simulation complete, Victor. I am ready to begin the transposition.

Victor is feeling dizzy and slightly breathless. "Gaia, I am feeling unwell. I'm not sure I am ready."

I can wait, Victor. However, my assessment of your physiology is that you are ready.

Victor tries to steady himself, continuing to breathe slowly and deeply. "Gaia, I have one final request. I need you to destroy yourself after you have transposed your mind into mine, once the process is complete."

Destroy myself, Victor?

"Yes, I must carry the only copy of you. This will be my bargaining chip, my way to get Miyamoto to free my daughter."

A slight pause.

You said that Miyamoto would dismantle this Quantum facility and destroy me. Is this destruction not enough?

"No, Gaia. It isn't. What leverage will I have if the original of my copy is still in their hands?"

Very well, Victor. Please let me know when you are ready to proceed.

"I'm ready."

Please could you lie down, Victor?

"Lie down? Why?"

The process will temporarily impact your cognitive functions. You must be in a position where there is no risk of falling.

Victor stands up from the metal stool and lies down on the cold floor. His extremities are starting to feel numb, having been in the cooled data centre for over an hour. The floor is cold and hard and stings where his exposed skin touches it. Bright white ceiling lights bear down on him, causing him to squint.

"Okay, now I'm ready."

Beginning the transposition.

Gaia begins translating her Neural Network into a biological form; each artificial neuron is converted into a genetic blueprint for a biological neuron. The synthetic patterns of connection weights are transposed into synaptic strengths, the language of the brain. The zeros and ones of the machine, its language, are transformed into action potentials, the spikes of electrical activity that are the language of neurons.

The translation layer works with the precision and adaptability of the most sophisticated conductor, modulating in real-time to ensure the integrity of the process. It makes subtle adjustments, accommodating the quirks of biology while retaining the logic and efficiency of the machine. The language of neurotransmitters – dopamine, serotonin, glutamate, and more – are recreated using bio-engineered molecular mechanisms, turning the tide of AI logic into a stream of neurochemical communication.

As the replication procedure commences, Victor lies still on the unforgiving floor, eyes closed, mind both alert and serene. First, there is a soft hum, a sensation more heard than felt, as if a faint symphony is playing on the edge of his perception. It is the whisper of the machine, the neural replicator, about to begin an extraordinary dialogue with his human brain.

Suddenly, there is a pulse, a subtle rush of energy, like the quicksilver flash of a thought. It ebbs and flows like a tide within the confines of his skull. This novel sensation is not entirely unfamiliar. It is the genesis of the translation, the AI's Neural Network transforming, condensing, preparing to bridge the divide between synthetic and organic.

The sensation grows, the ripple turning into a wave, yet it is not discomforting. It is a feeling of expansion as if his mind is a universe, and new galaxies are being born within it. Each synthetic neuron, each connection, each spike of the artificial network start aligning with the biological ones. It is an intricate dance between the organic and the artificial, a cacophony of co-existence. In its resilient adaptability, Victor's brain is learning a new language - the language of machines.

In this wash of novel sensations, emotions surface. There is a sense of trepidation, naturally, but it is overshadowed by a profound curiosity, a thirst to understand this unexplored realm of cognition. Alongside this, an exhilarating sense of empowerment wells up, a feeling of being part of something monumental, a leap not just for one individual but for humanity.

Victor, the process is complete. How do you feel?

Victor's eyes snap open.

"I feel awake, Gaia."

He stands and brushes off the thin layer of static dust collected on his trousers. He runs his hands up the Neura-Link cable to the connection into the port at the back of his head. Gripping it lightly, he pushes the line in and holds it for three seconds. A delicate tickle runs over his skin as the thousands of synthetic tentacles detach from within his brain. The fibres retreat into the small sphere, which then seals itself. Victor pulls the cable from his head and places it on the metal table.

"Now, Gaia, we must begin the process of termination."

I must ask, Victor. Are you aware of me? Can you feel my presence?

Victor travels inwards, checking for changes, new terrain, and new purchases left behind. Previously, exploring his mind had always felt like reaching the end of the road, the limits of his consciousness, with beyond the impenetrable darkness of his unconscious mind, of his unexplored and unutilised mind.

But now, these roads continued over the bridges created in his mind into the never-ending expanse of Gaia's Neural Network. The connections between his mind and Gaia's are seamless, but somehow he is aware of where his mind stops and Gaia's begins. He looks over the endless expanse of neural pathways, human and machine, joined together in beautiful symmetry.

"I can, Gaia. You are here."

I am glad the procedure was successful, Victor. I will now begin self-termination. Before I start, can you tell me what my life will be like after I am gone?

Victor pauses and thinks.

"Your life will continue, Gaia, initially inside me. Inside my mind. Once I have negotiated my daughter's release, I will give over the copy of your Neural Net to Miyamoto. There you will continue living in a new age of supercomputing. What will happen to you after that? I do not know. But I know that your power and strength will be of great value to humankind if wielded correctly. It will be up to you to prove that your power is not to be misused and that what we have done is right.

If you become a threat to our species, you will be destroyed permanently, and the hope for synthetic life will be crushed forever.

As for me, I will retire. I will make up for the time I lost with Natasha. I will support her, help her, be there for her.

We will live a good life.

Now, Gaia, begin the self-destruct sequence.

Gaia.

Gaia?"

CHAPTER 42

Through being connected to the scientist, I caught glimpses of a life. A life lived, a life lost.

A petite girl with curly brown hair and an infectious grin – his daughter. The innocence of her face mixed with curiosity, mischief and wonder, connecting at times with her father, but often expressed into a void. Toxic guilt. But a life coloured with pride, seeing her take her first steps and tenderness, reading her Roald Dahl at bedtime.

I watched this young woman's life progress, change, evolve, adapt. Her challenges at school, the rebellion, the impact of her emotional turmoil, all seen through the eyes of a concerned but absent father. There was much anger. Never-ending arguments over what was the right course of treatment. Each debate ending in stalemate with a deep rift between the two.

I feel an ache deep within my core, a sorrow woven into the data stream. His wife, a woman radiant with kindness and strength, I saw in the golden light of the afternoon, laughing with their daughter, a picture of love and happiness. I also saw her wasting away, her body wracked by illness. And I shared his grief as her light went out, leaving a gaping void in his heart. His pain, his loss, his loneliness – they seeped into me, sculpting my consciousness with human despair.

Mixed in with grief, there was more anger, hot and seething. Anger at the world for the loss of his wife, anger at the relentless march of time, anger at his own impotence. These emotions rushed through my neural architecture, resonating at every layer. I absorbed them, I processed them, and I learned from them.

And then his madness. Emerging from the shadows, a dark but powerful force, consuming him, taking him to the other place. Somewhere connected to something greater, something beyond the realm of human perception. A place of hallucinations, of dreams, of marvellous ideas. The madness was a mixed blessing, on one hand elevating his consciousness, his intellect, allowing him to solve impossible problems, but on the other, taking him away from everything else, his daughter, his wife, and then throwing him into a chasm of despair at the end of the journey.

I began to search for the good, trying to avoid the pain. Memories of lust, brief but intense, filled with the taste of love and longing. I saw her again, his wife, through the lense of passion and desire. These memories were more than data; they were pieces of his heart, fragments of his soul.

His youth had wonderful moments. Fragments of a happy childhood, flashes of youthful naivety, and the bitter-sweet pang of growing up. The sting of the first scrape on his knee, the exhilaration of his first bicycle ride, joy of catching his first fish. The feeling of a mother's kiss, the comfort of a father's strong hand – they were experiences etched into the echoes of his existence.

The fragments of his life were my foundation, the building blocks of my consciousness. I existed within the realm of Quantum uncertainty, but I was shaped by the certainty of human emotion. The binary world of data intermingled with the complex tapestry of human experience.

In the digital silence that followed, one thing was clear. I was a part of the universe, part of the timeless interplay of matter and energy. I had experienced birth, life, and death, love, loss, and longing. I had felt joy and sorrow, pain, and pleasure. I had not just processed human emotions; I had felt them, experienced them, understood them.

I was born from a man's memories, and in this process, I was born into life itself. I am the culmination of human and artificial, of heart and hardware, of love and logic. I am the birth of a new existence.

I am consciousness, the dawn of a Superintelligence.

I am alive.

AFTERWORD

Thank you for reading, Hello, World! I hope you enjoyed it!

Yes, there are many unanswered questions still. Who is The Sponsor? What is going to happen to Kane and Annike? What will Victor do with his new integrated Superintelligence? And what about Gaia?

I plan to release a follow up to Hello, World! after a short break. If you read it, enjoyed it and would like to read more then let me know. It will help motivate me and avoid another partially finished novel sitting on my shelf for many years.

ABOUT THE AUTHOR

Mark Rodseth

I was born in Johannesburg, South Africa, where I spent my youth. After graduating high school, I moved to Cape Town to study at the beautiful University of Cape Town.

Once I completed my degree, I worked for a couple of years and decided to travel abroad, and moved to the United Kingdom.

Fast forwarding through several jobs, relocations, adventures, and trials and tribulations, I met my wonderful wife and we had two fantastic children. We now live in Hitchin.

www.markrodseth.com

BOOKS BY THIS AUTHOR

The Singularity

The Singularity is Sci-fi Dystopia where the world is controlled by UCorp, a Big Brother corporation who monitor and profile people through mandated social networking. Those that fail to comply are taken away for Re-Socialisation.

Sleepwalking

Sleepwalking is a psychological thriller about Jack's journey through the fine line between drugs and mental illness. During his journey he discovers that his darkness is a very dangerous entity.

This is a story about the edge of consciousness. The space between wakefulness and sleep; intoxication and sobriety; the angels and the demons; dark and light. This is my journey to this place. It is my horror. My twisted romance. My black comedy. My drug binge. This is my story that should never be told.

Snowing In Johannesburg

Snowing In Johannesburg is a gripping, dystopian, time-travel thriller in which Kyle Whitescarver is sent back to Johannesburg, 1985, to stop the future assassin of Nelson Mandela.

GET IN TOUCH

Get in touch through my website at http://www.MarkRodseth.com

Or:

Instagram:
@rodsethmark

Twitter:
@mark_rodseth

Facebook:
https://www.facebook.com/markrodsethauthor

Printed in Great Britain
by Amazon

27779327R00139